Please turn the page for more reviews. . . .

"Bochco knows a thing or two about storytelling and character, and his book rips gleefully along. The characters shoot sparks when they bounce off each other, and Bochco has a way of working in jokes that are really funny—as well as indicative of his affection for Hollywood."
—*Seattle Times/Post-Intelligencer*

"A nasty little novel, and an amusing one. . . . This is also a fun read, partly because Bochco himself is probably a funny guy, and because he quotes several funny old stories about Hollywood and its citizens."
—*San Jose Mercury News*

"Good fun . . . This one has *insider* written all over it. . . . Bochco stage-manages the plot trickery effectively, and he makes the most of his crotchety narrator."
—*Booklist*

"It is obvious . . . that Bochco understands how 'the business' works. . . . The sting of truth."
—*Los Angeles Times*

Books published by The Ballantine Publishing Group are available at quantity discounts on bulk purchases for premium, educational, fund-raising, and special sales use. For details, please call 1-800-733-3000.

DEATH BY
HOLLYWOOD

a novel

STEVEN BOCHCO

BALLANTINE BOOKS • NEW YORK

A Fawcett Book
Published by The Random House Publishing Group

www.ballantinebooks.com

ISBN 0-345-46687-X

Manufactured in the United States of America

First Random House Hardcover Edition: September 2003
First Fawcett Mass Market Edition: March 2004

OPM 10 9 8 7 6 5 4 3 2 1

FOR MY BELOVED WIFE, DAYNA,
WHO HAS ALWAYS BELIEVED IN ME,
EVEN WHEN I DIDN'T

DEATH BY
HOLLYWOOD

CHAPTER 1

THERE USED TO BE A WRITER BY THE NAME OF MERLE
Miller, who wrote that people in Hollywood are
always touching you—not because they like you,
but because they want to see how soft you are before they eat you alive. He was right. It's a tough
town and a tough business, and if you don't watch
your step, either one'll kill you, which I guess is
what this story is actually about.

By way of formal introduction, my name is Eddie
Jelko, and I'm an agent. I represent screenwriters,
primarily, and a few important directors. I used to
represent actors when I first started in the business
almost twenty years ago, but it didn't take me long
to figure out that actors are crazy. They tend to be
paranoid, narcissistic, and, in general, oblivious to
the needs and feelings of others. The good news is,
they can also be charming, seductive, charismatic,

and, in the case of the very few, so genuinely gifted that simply being in their presence is a privilege. That said, celebrity, for the ego-challenged, can be as destructive as heroin. A little is too much, as they say, and too much is never enough.

In my naïveté, I thought writers and directors would be different. Fat chance. They're just as loony. In fact, the entertainment industry as a whole is one giant dysfunctional family. Everyone's terrified—of their own failure, or of everyone else's success—and as a general rule, you can assume that everyone lies about everything. (Have you ever looked at an actor's résumé—at the bottom, under SPECIAL SKILLS? Speaks three languages. Black belt in martial arts. Rides horses and motorcycles. Juggling and acrobatics. The truth is, you're lucky if they can drive a fucking car.)

And agents? By and large, we're nothing more than well-paid pimps who represent our pooched-out clients as if they're beautiful young virgins, offering them up to a bunch of jaded johns who know better, but these are the only whores in town. As the saying goes, denial is not a river in Egypt. It's a river in Hollywood, and it runs deep, and brown.

The story I want to tell you involves, among other things, a screenwriter whose career is fading out more than it's fading in, a billionaire's wife, and a murder—which means, of course, there's also a cop. Plus, the story has one other thing going for it. It's true.

Would I lie to you?

CHAPTER 2

IT STARTS AT THE GRILL, IN BEVERLY HILLS, ON A BREATH-
lessly hot September day, and if you've never been
there, or if you've spent the last ten years or so on
Mars, the Grill is *the* place to go for lunch if you
want to eyeball a Who's Who of the biggest power
brokers in Hollywood. It's a bright, friendly room
with white walls, lots of dark wood, and green
leather banquettes, a bar on the left as you walk in,
and a long row of booths going all the way to the
back of the room on your right. These are the
power tables, and if Michael, the maître d' and
manager, puts you at one of them, you can rest as-
sured your place in the pantheon of Hollywood Big
Boys is secure. On any given day you can see the
likes of Barry Diller, Brian Grazer, or Brad Grey, to
name a few familiar names. Star sightings are also
not uncommon. Last week, for instance, on the

same day, I saw Sophia Loren *and* Anthony Hopkins.

You'll also run into most of the top lawyers and agents in the film and television business—guys who aren't necessarily household names but who wield enormous clout in the industry. Let's just say if a Palestinian suicide bomber blew himself up in the Grill at one-fifteen on a Thursday afternoon, he'd probably take half the Jews and three quarters of the heaviest hitters in town with him. I'm exaggerating, but you get my meaning.

Anyway, I'm sitting in a booth here at the Grill waiting for my client Bobby Newman to show up. Typically, he's late. I call it Newman Standard Time.

Bobby's a screenwriter, and I invited him to lunch to read him the riot act. He was supposed to turn in a first-draft screenplay to the producer, Brian Grazer, almost six weeks ago (the studio is getting extremely impatient, as this isn't the first time he's stiffed them). Brian is threatening to breach his deal, and I'm getting sick to death of making up bullshit excuses for him. I've got to do business with these people on behalf of a couple of dozen other clients, and I'm starting to lose my credibility (which, coming from an agent, might sound like an oxymoron, with the emphasis on the moron part, but let's face it—if you lose your credibility in Hollywood, what've you got left?).

As long as I'm waiting, I may as well tell you a little about Bobby. He grew up a mama's boy on the Upper East Side of Manhattan, in extremely comfortable financial circumstances. He was the kind of smart-ass kid who'd turn you in for passing around dirty pictures in class. When he was eleven years old, four sixth-graders cornered him in the school bathroom and held him down, and each boy dropped his pants and sat on little Bobby's face. You'd like to think that, after what the other kids did to him in the bathroom, Bobby went out, pumped up at the gym, learned to fight, and individually sought out each kid and beat the shit out of him. If you were writing it (which, I suppose you could argue, is what Bobby's been doing ever since), that's what you'd want to see. The trouble is, you don't get to invent your life, at least not when you're eleven, and more often than not, if you're the kind of kid who's a candidate for an ass facial to begin with, it usually paralyzes you with fear for the rest of your life.

The situation wasn't helped any by the fact that Bobby's mother yanked him out of school that very day, enrolled him in an even more expensive private school the day after, and filed a lawsuit the day after *that*, which the school quickly and quietly settled out of court to the tune of about a hundred thousand dollars, which, unbeknownst to their benefactors, they siphoned out of the scholarship fund.

In his early adolescence, Bobby lost himself in books, and by the time he was fifteen, having grown into a pretty good-looking kid, girls and drugs (pot, mostly) took over, and he started to write short stories about teenage angst. (One of them, entitled "Jew Boy," was about a kid who's assaulted in a school bathroom by four toughs who take turns sitting on his face. He actually submitted it to *The New Yorker,* and got the standard rejection letter.)

By the time he was a high school senior, he was writing screenplays as well, and because he was sleeping with a girl who wanted to go to NYU film school, Bobby applied too, and got in. Of course, the relationship didn't survive the first semester, and Bobby wound up marrying another girl he met there, from L.A., whose stepfather was a big-shot entertainment lawyer. The day he graduated was the day he headed west to seek his fame and fortune in Hollywood.

The new wife's stepfather got him a job in the mail room at CAA, the marriage lasted all of eighteen months, but by the time it petered out, Bobby was already entrenched. He had a job during the day and, loaded on weed, wrote scripts at night. CAA fired him when they found out he'd submitted a low-budget screenplay to Roger Corman under a forged cover letter from a CAA agent who had no idea who the hell Bobby Newman even was.

You can probably guess what the punch line to *that* story is. Corman bought the script, and next thing Bobby knew, the agency that had fired him was now the agency representing him. By the time Bobby was thirty, he was making a damn good living as a script doctor, rewriting scripts weak on dialogue and/or story, and, in spite of the fact that he liked to party too much, he maintained a pretty disciplined work schedule.

It was about that time that he had a falling out with his agent at CAA about the quality of the assignments he was getting. I'd been shamelessly courting Bobby for over a year, encouraging him to stop thinking of himself as a script doctor and telling him he'd earned the right to move up to the A-list of writers that studios go to with their most important projects.

The year before, I'd changed agencies myself. Like Bobby, I'd started my career in the mail room of a big talent agency. There's no shortage of mail room war stories testifying to what a cutthroat environment it is, so I won't bore you with mine, other than to tell you it compares with the way sled dogs are treated in northern Canada to determine who the alpha males are. (They chain the dogs to a fence with just enough separation so they can't kill each other but close enough so that the snarling, teeth-baring alpha dogs can intimidate the shit out of their more timid fencemates. By a process of elimination, you can pretty quickly determine the lead dog, and if you're not the lead dog, as they say, the view never changes.)

Suffice it to say, the mail room where I got my early training was a dog-eat-dog world. (I think it was that famous alpha male Sam Goldwyn who added, "And no dog's gonna eat me.")

One of the fundamental problems with working in a big agency is that you often find yourself trapped in conflicts of interest—not so much yours as your clients'.

Let's say, for instance, you represent a young first-time screenwriter who's written a tender, sensitive love story. And let's say, too, that your agency's unhappiest client is some big-shot macho action-adventure type director whose last two movies tanked and he's blaming—who else?—his agents. Further, he decides that the way to resuscitate his failing career is to go for a complete change of pace and direct—you guessed it—a tender, sensitive love story. You think Mr. Big Shot's not going to get first crack at your young writer's material, regardless of whether he's the right director for this particular project or not? Do you think the fact that it might not be in the young writer's best interests is of any concern to the agency, given that it perceives its primary obligation to be servicing the needs of its higher-profile client, even if it's at the expense of your young first-time writer?

That, ladies and gentlemen, is your classic conflict of interest, and as an agent, I'd gotten weary of my client's welfare sucking hind tit, as it were, to my employer's.

And because the small but prestigious agency I'm now a partner of always defines its own interests as being those of its clients, I didn't have to blow a lot of smoke up Bobby Newman's ass to get him to dump his agent and sign with me. All I had to do was ask him if he was happy with the attention he was getting and suggest that if he wasn't, a small boutique agency with a blue-chip client roster as short as his grocery list might be more suited to his needs.

Bobby's former agents didn't talk to me for a couple of years, but it's the old story: the jilted wife always blames the other woman for stealing her husband. It never occurs to her that she may have had something to do with driving the poor slob away in the first place. (Speaking of infidelity, did you ever stop to wonder why wives always blame the other woman but husbands always blame their wives?)

After Bobby signed with me, I got him to focus not only on style but on substance as well. He seemed to have a real talent for hard-boiled action-adventure characters, so I encouraged him to develop that aspect of his talent, since that was the kind of writing most producers were looking for. I mean, let's face it—Joel Silver wasn't going to buy a movie about a talking dog who becomes president of the United States—which happened to be a story Bobby wanted me to peddle to Disney. I told him I didn't think it was a very good idea and that, besides, it wasn't the kind of stuff I wanted him wasting his time on. I suppose I pissed him off, because he didn't talk to me for a couple of weeks or so, but at least he knew I'd tell him the truth, right or wrong. And I guess he came to respect my opinion finally, because to my knowledge, he never finished writing the dog thing and never mentioned it again.

Under my guidance, it didn't take long before Bobby got to the point where he was making a high-six-figure income annually, he'd bought the Hollywood house, and had met his current wife, Vee. Within a year, they were married. He'd made it. He was in the game, and it was his game to lose . . .

Anyway, Bobby finally shows up around twelve forty-five and slides into the booth, telling the waiter he'd like a bottle of the Vine Cliff Chardonnay please, put it in a bucket. Jesus Christ, it's twelve forty-five, he knows I don't drink in the daytime, and he's ordering not a glass but a whole goddamn *bottle* of the stuff without even consulting a wine list. He probably has it memorized. And forget about hello-how-are-you or anything even remotely resembling a civilized greeting.

He's barely squirmed his ass into the booth when he starts right off with: "I know you're pissed as hell, but I swear to God I've only got twenty more pages to write, I'll turn it in by the end of the week."

To which I say, "If you've written twenty pages *total,* I'll kiss your ass in Macy's window," and immediately Bobby drops the bullshit.

"I'm fucked," he says. "I got writer's block. I keep rewriting the same six pages over and over again. Every night I lie in bed, I haven't gotten a decent night's sleep in months, I promise I'm not going to even look at 'em, I'm just going to jump ahead to the next scene, and every morning I go to the fucking computer and start all over again. Plus, Vee and I are having these horrible fights, it gets me so upset I start drinking."

And, as if on cue, the waiter returns with the bottle of wine, and while he's opening it and pouring it out, Bobby tells me, without irony, that he's drinking so much every night it takes him half the morning just to get his head far enough out of his ass to start writing.

Seeing Bobby on the ropes and hoping to lift his

spirits, I reach down for a fat manila envelope lying beside me on the banquette and hand it to him. "Read this," I say.

"What is it?"

"It's Jared Axelrod's next film, it starts shooting six weeks from now in Prague, and it needs a rewrite, which I told him you could deliver in three weeks. You're meeting him tomorrow at two-thirty."

I say this to Bobby with as much matter-of-fact understatement as I can muster, given the fact that I had to beg Axelrod to take the meeting. And then, because I think it's important to impress Bobby with the urgency of his situation, I also tell him that maybe it'd be nice to get a quick payday before the shit hits the fan on the assignment he's currently pissing down a sinkhole, along with what's left of his career.

Does he thank me? Fat fucking chance. All he does is obsess over how I can think he's capable of rewriting someone else's piece of shit when he can't even get past page six of his own piece of shit. I suggest to him that maybe working on something fresh, something he's not emotionally involved in, will actually be good for him. "Get a little positive reinforcement," I say. "Actually meet a deadline for a change, put a quick hundred and fifty thousand in the bank—where's the downside?"

"The truth is, I'm scared," Bobby says miserably, and by now he's on his third glass of wine. "I bomb out on a lousy three-week rewrite, I'm totally fucked."

"The *truth* is," I tell him, "if you don't get this screenplay finished by the end of the week, we're *both* fucked."

So that was lunch.

CHAPTER 3

AFTER BOBBY LEAVES THE GRILL, HE WALKS OVER TO the public parking garage on Rodeo Drive to get his car. (Actually, strictly speaking, the parking lot is *under* Rodeo and it's free, with valet parking, for the first two hours. Can you believe it? Beverly Hills. What a country.)

If Bobby had half a brain, he'd've taken the time to walk off the two thirds of a bottle of wine he drank (if I'd drunk that much, I'd've passed out on the sidewalk). Instead, he retrieves his Boxster, throws the script I gave him into the passenger seat, and, with the top down, speeds up the ramp and out into traffic, nearly running down three Japanese tourists in the process.

You won't be surprised when I tell you that within three minutes Bobby's being pulled over on Little Santa Monica Boulevard by a Beverly Hills motorcycle cop. What may surprise you is that while the cop's writing him up ("You're being cited for making an unsafe lane change, Bob"), he sees his wife, Vee, across the street necking with some guy right out in front of the Peninsula Hotel. Un-fucking-believable. They can't keep their hands off each other, the guy's saying something in her ear, she's laughing, he's grabbing at her ass, and while Bobby watches, dumbstruck, they disappear into the hotel together.

If you ever needed an excuse not to write, there's one right there.

"Fucking *cock*sucker," Bobby says out loud, and the only good news is, the cop writing him up is too far behind the Boxster to hear him say it, otherwise my afternoon would've been devoted to bailing him out of the Beverly Hills clink (where, to the best of my knowledge, there is no underground valet parking, free or otherwise).

Anyway, Bobby gets home in an understandably dark mood, opens up another bottle of wine (there's a shocker), and goes into his office to read the script I gave him. It's called *Fathers and Daughters,* it's written by a woman named Mimi Webster (who I happen to also represent), and it's a story about this guy Jonathan, in his late fifties, good-looking, suc-cessful, married for the second time to a beautiful and successful woman (Caroline) for twenty years. He's got two grown children from his first mar-riage, and Caroline has a twenty-seven-year-old daughter from her first marriage. The daughter,

Heather, has a troubled marriage of her own that's beginning to teeter.

Caroline gets diagnosed with cancer, which it turns out she's had a while but was in total denial about, and by the time it's discovered, it's too late. It's spread all over the place, and pretty quickly she goes out of the picture. Literally. It's a tragic loss for Jonathan, and though his friends try to help him through his grief, he's inconsolable.

Caroline's daughter, Heather, struggling with her own demons, is also devastated by the loss of her mother. And so, Heather and Jonathan, each for different reasons, are drawn together by the pain of loss and loneliness. For him, Heather is like the good daughter he lost years earlier when he divorced his first wife, instead of the daughter who bitterly resented him for leaving her mom. And for Heather, who was raised mostly by her real father and his new wife, Jonathan's the father figure who can identify with her loss and share her grief.

You can pretty much figure where it goes from there: the relationship deepens to the point where they both realize they're in love with each other. Jonathan is obsessed by the profound similarities between his dead wife and her beautiful young daughter, and Heather feels guilty and conflicted competing against the memory of her mother for Jonathan's love and affection. The sexual tension between them is agonizing, but the guilt they feel scares them both off.

Finally, they agree they have to get away from

each other. He goes off to Europe, and she renews her efforts to put her failing marriage back together. Needless to say, the marriage goes *pffft,* Heather jets off to—where else?—Prague to hook up with Jonathan, and, notwithstanding the obvious difficulties they know they'll have to endure, they give in to their feelings. Music swells, fadeout, not a dry eye in the house.

If you like that kind of movie, fine. It is what it is. But I think what Jared Axelrod's looking for is something a little edgier, tone-wise. Or, as he put it to me, more *muscular*—which is a current favorite term of producers when describing their material. And the reason I was able to sell him on meeting with Bobby is that Bobby's always basically worked in the action-adventure genre, he's generally pretty fast (or at least he used to be), his characters tend to be tough, macho guys, and his dialogue is, well, *muscular.*

The idea being, in principle, that you get the women in the tent because of the romance and you get the guys to come along because the male lead is tough, hard-nosed but, underneath it all, sensitive. Think Harrison Ford trying to hold off boning Gwyneth Paltrow because he knows it's wrong, and you get the drift.

Anyway, it's about four o'clock in the afternoon, Bobby's halfway through the script, and Vee comes dragging in, saying she spent the afternoon shlepping from studio to studio, auditioning for various roles in *Judging Amy, E.R.,* and *The Guardian.* Typically, Bobby doesn't ask how it went. Instead, he gestures to the bottle of wine. "You want a glass?"

Vee says, "Okay, let me just take a shower and change into sweats first."

Maybe if Bobby isn't half-bagged (what else is new), he confronts her right then and there about what she's doing outside the Peninsula Hotel playing grab-ass in public with some asshole in an Armani suit. But he is, so he doesn't. Maybe because he's afraid that instead of being all remorseful and guilty, she'll tell him, *au contraire*, she *loves* fucking this other guy, he touches her in all the right places, he takes his goddamn time about it, he waits till she comes, then he gently works her around till she comes again. Plus, Bobby doesn't need to hear from her (again) how on those rare occasions when he *does* express an interest in making love, he can't even get the little bastard to stay up (which the Prozac might have something to do with).

I realize it's easy to think Vee's a promiscuous, cheating bitch or that I don't like her, neither of which is true. This is not to say I approve of her behavior; I don't. But let's face it. Being married to Bobby Newman is no picnic. He's self-absorbed. He has serious bouts of depression. You already know he drinks too much. Plus, he can be hostile and manipulative when he's not being an emotionally withholding prick. I also know for a fact that while he may love Vee, he also takes her for granted, belittles her career aspirations, and generally doesn't take the time to display the little gestures of affection that make a person feel special, loved, or desired.

I also know for a fact that she's begged him, on more than one occasion, to go see a shrink with her, which Bobby flat-out refused to do. He also recently quit taking his Prozac, on the grounds that it was dulling his writing edge (to which I say *what* writing edge, but that's another story).

So while you're thinking about Vee cheating on her husband, also think about how she's a thirty-two-year-old woman with legitimate needs that her husband, for one reason or another, is neither willing nor able to satisfy.

By now you're also probably asking yourself, How come she didn't just leave him if he's such an asshole? It's a fair question, particularly when you're asking it about someone else's marriage and not your own. I'm no shrink, but I've been around the block a few times myself, marriage-wise and otherwise, and I think the answer is, people get scared. Scared of divorce. Scared of losing their money or their social standing. Scared of being alone. Or maybe sometimes they just don't think they deserve any better than what they've got and they'd rather be in a shitty relationship than no relationship at all.

And then there's sex.

It's my own personal observation, at least as far as men are concerned, that sex is the great broken promise of marriage. This is not to imply that men only get married for sex or that they don't get sex after they're married. But for *most* guys, it's not just the sex per se but the *idea* of sex. You know, *sexy* sex. The kind of sex where you're doing it in the car, in the shower, on the floor, and it's like you can't get enough of each other, which is what being in love is all about. It's why you ask her to marry you in the first place, because you can't remember it ever being like this with anyone else in your whole life and you never want it to stop, and then you get married and . . . it stops. Not right away maybe. But gradually, it stops. Her see-through nightgowns disappear. She doesn't put on the sexy underwear for you to take off her, or wear makeup to bed to make love. Maybe because it's not new anymore. Or because it's not forbidden. Or maybe because the reality of life—kids, jobs, money, bills, in-laws—gets in the way of the kind of spontaneous sex I'm talking about. Whatever the reason, sex—the kind of sex men leave their wives and marry other women for—almost always disappears over time. I don't mean to be crude here, but do the math. How many times did your wife let you come in her mouth before you were married versus how many times after?

I'm not suggesting that women don't have their own issues when it comes to the men they marry, or their own deep feelings of having been cheated out of legitimate expectations. And I'm sure that their reasons for feeling cheated, or unfulfilled, are no less legitimate than the guys' are. My only point is, people who shouldn't be married stay married all the time, for all sorts of reasons, and one of the ways they manage to do it is by never telling each other the truth and never confronting each other honestly about their fears, resentments, and desires. Which means, of course, that all those fears, resentments, and desires harden into nasty, unforgiving, poison-tipped arrows that they carry around in their quivers, just waiting for the right moment to whip one out and fire it into their loved one's cold, cheating heart.

As I said, I'm no shrink, and I'm in way over my head talking about shit like this, but I wanted you to know a little bit about Vee so you wouldn't think she's just another airhead actress with phony tits who married a screenwriter, hoping he'd open the door to a career for her.

Because, for openers, her tits *aren't* phony, which I guess puts her in the one half of one percent of all women in Hollywood who *haven't* had their tits enlarged.

And as long as we're on the subject of tits, what's up with these women, anyway? Have they all gone nuts? Do they think people can't tell they have water balloons stuck up under their chest walls? Don't they realize that they all look alike? That every person, man or woman, takes one look at them and knows immediately that they have implants, the same way you can always tell a guy who's wearing a rug? Doesn't it matter to them that their nipples are constantly poking out like pencil erasers and that their breasts don't move around under their shirts when they walk? Or that when they lie on their back, their tits shoot straight up in the air like a pair of Titan surface-to-air missiles? I guess they don't care because men don't care. They'd rather grab a handful of phony tit than no tit at all.

In any event, one of the great things about Vee is, she's maybe the only woman I ever met who genuinely, unself-consciously seems to like her body as is. Of course, what's not to like? She's about five-eight, 125 pounds or so, with great legs, terrific breasts—not huge, but really nicely shaped, and they're 100 percent real—and the kind of ass you try not to spend too much time looking at, because it'd be rude, but you do anyway. Plus, she's cute. Not beautiful exactly, but not your standard American pretty, either, with blond hair, bright blue eyes, a sexy, full-face smile showing teeth just uneven enough that you know they're real, too. If I were to give you an image to compare her against, I'd say think Meg Ryan, ten years ago.

Perhaps now you have a little more sense of the woman Bobby follows into the bedroom, glass of wine in hand, watching as she undresses. Shoes, skirt, blouse, down to her sexy little bra and thong panties, and when those come off, Bobby picks them up off the floor and smells them.

"You're disgusting," Vee says.

"Thank you," Bobby says back, following her into the bathroom, watching as, naked now, she leans into the stall and turns on the shower faucets. And even half-drunk, angry and humiliated as he is, he can't help admiring her physical beauty, which he experiences as an ache. But instead of taking the opportunity to tell her he loves her, that he knows their marriage is fucked-up and he wants to try and fix it before it's too late—in other words, instead of taking the direct approach, which at least would've been the grown-up thing to do—he tries to goad her into a fight by suggesting he's kind of sweaty, too, and how about he jumps into the shower with her for a game of Lather the Lizard.

"I'm not in the mood for Lather the Lizard," Vee says, climbing into the shower. "I just want to get cleaned up, have a nice cold glass of wine, and get relaxed."

"You're always complaining we never have sex. Here I'm offering myself up and suddenly *you're* the one not interested. What's up with that?"

By now, the steam is billowing out of the shower stall and water is spraying the front of Bobby's clothes. "All right," Vee says, giving in. "Take your clothes off and get in."

"Never mind," Bobby says. "I don't need a mercy fuck."

See, that's how the really bad fights start between people. Because now Vee says, "What is the *matter* with you? Why are you like this?" which immediately takes things from the specific issue of are they going to fuck in the shower or not to the more general issue of their free-floating anger toward each other, and once you go there, watch out.

Predictably, like the dance that it always is, Bobby says, "Why am *I* like this? Why am *I* like this? Why am I like *what*?"

"Like, I don't know—like so fucking hostile all the time."

"Did it ever occur to you maybe I'm so fucking

hostile because you never show me any fucking affection, or express any fucking sympathy for the fact that I'm going through the worst miserable fucking time in my whole fucking career right now?"

"Oh, please."

"Ever hear the concept, I love you, Bobby, let's take a shower together, instead of me always having to feel like a fucking beggar?"

"I'm not a mind reader! If you want to fuck, *say* so," Vee shouts, trying to match Bobby's rising volume.

"Which is why I said let's take a shower!"

"And I said okay! And *you* said forget it!"

"Jesus Christ, this is where I came in," Bobby says. Now Vee starts to cry, as much out of frustration as from hurt. "Why are you doing this to me?"

"Right. It's always about you," Bobby says.

"Did it ever occur to you that maybe I'd feel like having sex more often if you actually did something productive once in a while instead of getting shit-faced at four o'clock in the afternoon and picking a fight?"

"Fuck you, Vee," Bobby says, and throws the contents of his wineglass at her crotch.

"You are such an asshole," Vee says, and slams the shower door shut on him.

"Maybe your boyfriend'll lick it off for you," Bobby says, and walks out of the bathroom, slamming the door behind him, not sure if she heard him or not and not wanting to stick around to find out.

CHAPTER 4

THE NEXT MORNING, BOBBY WAKES UP ON THE COUCH, dehydrated and hungover, and by the time he's chewed three aspirins and taken a hot shower, Vee's headed out the door, her voice as cold as a well-digger's ass, informing Bobby she's going over to Paramount for an audition.

And because writers like to torture themselves, Bobby quickly gets dressed and drives over to the Peninsula Hotel, where he parks across the street, waiting an hour and a half till he sees his wife exiting the hotel with the same guy from the day before, watching them as they kiss and grab-ass each other good-bye.

The toughest part of finding out your wife is cheating on you is not being able to get the picture of it out of your head. You see them in your mind's eye making love, your wife—your fucking *wife,* for

God's sake!—opening her legs to this prick, saying intimate things in his ear, touching his body, touching his cock, doing things with him she won't do with you anymore. Or maybe never has.

You see him touching her, putting his hands on her, in her, all over her, invading *your* territory. And as each obsessive image mocks you, insults you, violates you, you experience what's commonly referred to as jealous rage, and you realize you're actually capable, in that moment, of murder. They used to call it a crime of passion, and under the right circumstances, no jury in the world would convict.

By way of example, there was a guy—this is years ago—named Jennings Lang, who was a big-shot talent agent at MCA (which later became Universal Studios in the days before the studio morphed into a multinational entertainment conglomerate).

Jennings Lang was supposedly having an affair with one of his clients, a beautiful movie star by the name of Joan Bennett, who was married to a producer named Walter Wanger. The story goes that Walter Wanger found out about the affair, confronted the two of them in flagrante delicto, as they say, pulled out a pistol, and shot off one of Jennings's balls.

Needless to say, he never spent a day in jail for what he did, and the guy who told me that story, a director named Jack Smight, swore to me that from that day on, he called Jennings *Jenning*.

Anyway, Bobby drives around nursing his jealous, obsessive rage, killing time until his two-thirty meeting with Jared Axelrod, and when he finally works his way through the Twentieth Century Fox studio security barricades at the front gate, parks his car halfway across the lot, and gets lost looking for this guy's bungalow, who do you think this Axelrod turns out to be?

If you guessed the guy his wife's been banging at the Peninsula Hotel, you'd be right. If you also guessed the meeting was a total disaster, that would be right, too.

For all the reasons I mentioned before about why I think Bobby didn't confront Vee, he's not about to confront Axelrod, either, particularly in front of Axelrod's development executive, a young, attractive woman named Lainie Ginsberg.

After several moments of strained amenities, while the assistant fetches Evian for everyone, Axelrod gets to it. "So. What'd you think of the script?"

Bobby now commences, predictably, to shoot himself in the foot. He tells Axelrod that the premise of the movie is bullshit and that the audience will be offended by the fact that this old guy is seducing his young stepdaughter. In the alternative, Bobby suggests the notion of turning the story into a less complicated emotional landscape by having the love interest be his dead wife's somewhat younger sister.

Now, even I know that's a terrible idea, and I represent the guy. But the real dynamic in the room has nothing to do with Bobby's ideas about Axelrod's script, good or bad. It has to do with the fact that Axelrod is fucking his wife. Bobby knows it— hell, Lainie Ginsberg probably knows it—and even though Axelrod doesn't know for sure whether Bobby knows it, off the hostile vibe emanating from Bobby, he suspects it. So, without being totally disrespectful (for obvious reasons), Axelrod, as nicely as he can, pisses all over Bobby's idea, saying maybe we'll get together on some other project sometime, I'm a big fan of your work, blah blah blah.

Of course, what Bobby probably *hears* is *I'm fucking your wife, you impotent third-rate hack. Now get the hell out of my office so I can laugh my ass off behind your back.*

At the door, Lainie Ginsberg offers Bobby her hand, telling him she's also a longtime admirer of his oeuvre. Bobby wants to say, Stick my oeuvre up your tight little Jewish ass, but instead he gives her a phony smile and beats it out of there.

About now, you're probably asking yourself why Bobby didn't just smack this guy in the mouth. I can't answer that one. Maybe he was afraid to alienate a guy everyone knows is gonna wind up running a studio within five years. Or maybe he was just so ashamed that he didn't want anyone to know his wife was screwing around behind his back with a movie producer who wouldn't even give him a lousy rewrite.

Whatever the case, when Bobby gets home, the first thing Vee says, as casually as she can, is, "How was your meeting?"

"The meeting was swell," Bobby says. "I asked him does he like fucking you from behind so he can watch his dick go in and out, or does he prefer being on the bottom so he can watch your tits bounce up and down?"

Vee hauls off and smacks Bobby in the face so hard it sounds like a gunshot. And from that point on, it's all over but the shouting. Bobby calls her a cheating cunt. Vee calls Bobby a loser—an impotent boozer who can't write his way out of a wineglass. He says he oughta throw her off the deck in back of the house (from where, by the way, you can see the HOLLYWOOD sign).

"Did you ever stop to ask yourself whose fault it is I'm having an affair?" Vee yells. "Can you remember the last time we went out for a meal together without having a fight? Or the last time you kissed me, or made love to me without me having to beg? Can you even remember the last time you were sober? Because I can't, and I finally couldn't take it anymore, and I was so lonely I would've fucked the pool man if we had one!"

"Well if you're so goddamn miserable," Bobby screams, "why don't you just pack up your shit and get the fuck out of my house," which is sort of like closing the barn door after the horse has already bolted, as she's already throwing stuff in an overnight bag, saying she should've left him months ago.

The sight of her actually packing suddenly breaks Bobby's heart, and all the fight goes out of him. "Come on, Vee, don't go, please," he begs. He even promises to go to the shrink with her, but he's a day late and a buck short. As afraid as she'd been, now that her secret's out, she feels liberated. Her fear, catalyzed by anger, has now turned to courage, and her sense of euphoria billows her sails and carries her out the door, leaving their marriage and Bobby, miserable and remorseful, in her wake.

I know all this because, coincidentally, I happened to call Bobby to ask him to meet me for drinks after work. I'd gotten an earful from Jared Axelrod about their meeting, and frankly, as much as I hated the idea, I realized I was going to have to fire Bobby as a client.

CHAPTER 5

OVER DRINKS AT THE BAR IN THE FOUR SEASONS HO-tel, Bobby tells me the whole story from A to Z, starting with getting pulled over by the motorcycle cop and seeing Vee across the street grabbing some guy's ass in front of the Peninsula Hotel to showing up for his meeting with Jared Axelrod and realizing he's the guy his wife's been banging.

"It's the worst meeting I ever took in my life," Bobby says. "If I didn't need the job so bad, I would've killed him on the spot."

Hindsight being twenty-twenty, I admit my tim-ing could have been better, but then again, is the timing ever right for bad things to happen to you? Is there ever a right time to find out your wife's cheating on you, or that someone you love has can-cer, or that Sherry Lansing at Paramount hates your script? I wasn't going to be doing Bobby—or for that matter myself—any favors by delaying the inevitable just because this happened to be the day his marriage broke up.

Plus, for whatever it's worth, no one has stuck by him longer than I have, to my own detriment, I might add, or defended him more loyally when everyone else was saying he'd lost his chops.

So, cutting to the chase, I tell Bobby that notwithstanding the fact that this is a horribly difficult time for him, I have to let him go as a client. Julius Caesar couldn't have looked any more stunned when Brutus stuck a knife in his kishkas.

"Are you kidding me?" he asks. "Is this like one of those sick doctor jokes, I have bad news and I have good news? The bad news is, your biopsy came back positive, you've got three weeks to live, but the good news is, as soon as you leave my office, I'm going to fuck my nurse?"

I try to explain to Bobby that this has been coming for months. I tell him I'll always be his friend, but I can't afford to have a guy like Jared Axelrod pissed off at me.

"This prick is screwing my wife and you're telling me you can't afford to have him pissed off at you? Are you serious?"

"I know you're upset," I say, "but try to see it from my point of view. I'm not saying he *isn't* a prick, but if I lose credibility with this guy, he'll start bad-mouthing me all over town. And then next thing you know, my calls aren't being returned, my other clients are being penalized because of it, *they* get pissed off at me, and before you know it, I'm persona non grata and my clients are getting picked off like grapes during crushing season. I mean, do the math: losing my credibility equals losing my clients equals losing my job. Suddenly I can't afford my kids' school, I can't make my mortgage payments, and my wife dumps me for Ron Perelman. I'm exaggerating for the sake of the point here, but credibility is the only thing I've got going for me in this business, and if I lose it, I may as well bend over, stick my head between my legs, and kiss my ass good-bye."

"What about integrity, fucko? What about friendship?"

"*Fucko?*" I say. "You have the balls to call *me* fucko? I have lied for you, I have advanced you money, I've been a friend and a shoulder for you to cry on, the words *thank you* have never passed your lips once in all the years I've represented you, and for all that I get called fucko? Well, fuck you, you self-absorbed piece of shit," I say, dropping a twenty on the bar and splitting before I *really* lose my temper.

I want to go on record saying I'm not unaware that agents have a shitty reputation. People say horrible things about us behind our backs, clients call us names right to our faces, and comedy writers make up nasty jokes about us, like the one about the gorgeous young actress who meets Mike Ovitz at a cocktail party.

"Omigod," she says to the *über*agent. "It's such an honor to meet you, Mr. Ovitz. You're the most powerful, sexy, charismatic man I've ever met, and

I'd like to take you into the guest bathroom, lock the door, and give you the most unbelievable blow job you've ever had in your whole life."

To which Ovitz says, "That's fine for you, but what's in it for me?"

Then there's the one about the agent who gets a call from a big-shot producer, asking what the agent thinks of his latest movie. The agent says, "Well, I gotta be honest. I didn't think it was your best work ever, the script wasn't all that good, and the actress who played the girlfriend of the lead really stunk up the room." Furious, the producer tells the agent that the actress who played the girlfriend happens to be his wife. "Wait a minute," the agent exclaims. "Let me finish!"

The point being, an agent's life is no tea party. Maybe not so much directors, but actors and writers are, by and large, big self-centered spoiled-rotten babies. Every one of their life's little disappointments winds up on our doorstep. And every job they don't get or every job they ever screwed up, whose fault is it? The agent's. You bust your ass trying to build a guy's career, he finally gets hot, and the first thing he does after he buys a new Mercedes is fire your ass and sign with some other agent, who's blowing smoke up *his* ass about what he can do for your client now that he's finally gotten the recognition he should've had years ago, blah blah blah . . .

That said, I still love writers. They're quirky, smart, fun to talk to, and often bizarre in their habits and lifestyles.

I once represented an East Coast writer who'd re-located to Los Angeles after I'd sold his first novel to Warner Bros. Not long after arriving, he showed up at my office early one morning, asking if I could advance him five thousand dollars against his first paycheck, due shortly. I wrote him my own personal check for the amount, and as promised, he paid me back within days. The following week, he asked again, and again I wrote him the check. This time, he paid me back in hundred-dollar bills. I don't know about you, but I don't see that kind of cash every day. (I have a producer friend who maintains that if you walked into every negotiation with a bag full of money and dumped it on the table, you could close most deals at a fraction of what they generally make for. Agents these days routinely close deals for millions of dollars, but can you imagine if you dumped, say, $750,000, *cash,* on some actor's coffee table? The IRS might be pissed off, but I bet the actor would love it.)

Anyway, when I asked my client where he got the cash, he told me with an embarrassed grin that he was commuting to Los Angeles every morning on the six A.M. flight from Las Vegas, where he'd taken up temporary residence at Caesars Palace. He'd write all day, catch an eight P.M. flight back to Vegas, stay up all night drinking and gambling and God knows what else, then show up in L.A. the next day, ready to work.

I had another writer once who I'd placed on staff at a hit TV show, and during a writers' meeting in the second-floor office of the executive producer, this writer—who'd been animatedly pitching a story to the entire staff (including one female)—at some point realized that a window washer had climbed a tall ladder outside the building and was squeegeeing the windows during his pitch. Without missing a beat, this writer stripped down to his boxer shorts, backed up to the window, whipped his shorts down around his knees, and pressed his bare ass up against the glass. The guys in the room were convulsed with laughter, and the female quit the next day.

And finally, I love writers because I don't think there's anything in the world that's scarier than staring at a blank page and reaching inside yourself for the inspiration it takes to put your fingers on the keys and make something out of nothing, knowing the whole time that when you're done, some idiot in a suit, with tons of opinions and no talent, will probably shit all over it. It takes courage, boys and girls, and courage is a fickle bitch at best.

Now that I've had time to reflect on it, I suppose I could've waited a day or two before dropping the hammer on Bobby. But I guess I did what I did because I felt so sorry for the poor bastard, and I was afraid that if I didn't do it right then and there, I wouldn't have the guts to do it at all . . .

CHAPTER 6

I T'S LATER THAT NIGHT, AND THE AIR TEMPERATURE IN the Hills is still in the high seventies, thanks to a blast furnace of a Santa Ana blowing in from the desert toward the ocean, leaving Hollywood a hot, glistening jewel under a shimmering, starlit sky. Bobby's wandering around his house barefoot, in boxers and a T-shirt, shell-shocked from the worst day of his entire adult life.

You can bet lots of men happily fantasize about dumping their wives, living large and single, picking and choosing from an endless supply of good-looking women dying to hook up with them. But the reality is, Bobby's never lived alone his whole adult life, and without Vee to animate it, the house not only feels empty but abandoned.

Half hating her, half missing her, hoping she'll call and knowing she won't, not even knowing where the hell she's gone, Bobby winds up ransacking her drawers and closets in a jealous rage, hoping he'll find evidence of her affair. He can't help torturing himself all over again with the image of her kneeling on the floor in the back of Axelrod's Mercedes, parked somewhere off Mulholland Drive, face down between his naked thighs, sucking the balls off him in the dark, then telling him how hot he makes her feel and how much she wants him.

In a life that's had its share of ups and, lately, more downs than the Dow Jones, this is the lowest Bobby's been yet, maybe ever, and he just makes it to the toilet before vomiting up all the wine he'd been drinking on an empty stomach.

CHAPTER 7

At the same time Bobby Newman is cleaning up his puke and changing into fresh clothes, two people are having sex in the master bedroom of a house not too far down the canyon from Bobby's. The man is a handsome Latino actor named Ramon, well built, in his mid-thirties, and the woman, Linda, is a dark-haired, white-skinned beauty with a knockout body, who, judging by the way she's sliding up and down Ramon's stiff dick, knows just what to do with it. Ramon's no slouch either, and if fucking were a spectator sport, these two would draw a hell of a crowd.

What's interesting about the two of them fucking, aside from the fact that watching attractive people fuck is always interesting, is that this scumbag Ramon is secretly taping the encounter with a video camera hidden inside the armoire facing the bed.

I suppose you could speculate about why Ramon likes to tape his sexual encounters, but one of the reasons I *know* he does it, at least in Linda's case, is to extort money from her, should it come to that. Ramon's been trying to get Linda to "lend" him a million dollars to start a production company, and she's been stringing him along, telling him she needs to talk to her husband, Marv, about it, but the truth is, she has no intention of ever talking to her husband about it, because she knows Ramon is a scumbag and her only interest in this guy lies south of the border.

And so it is, on this night, after a particularly athletic hour of sex, that Ramon presses his case for the money somewhat more aggressively than he has in the past, and Linda, with equal aggressiveness, tells him he ought to back off, that she doesn't like being pressured.

"You didn't mind the pressure the last hour or so, did you, baby," Ramon says, trying to play it off, but by now, Linda's tired of playing.

"Ramon, you're a good actor. You're a good teacher. You're a *great* lay. But I can't see talking Marv into investing a million dollars so you can suddenly be a Latin power player. It isn't gonna happen."

Ramon's not looking for a fight, not necessarily, so, nice as can be, he wonders what if he goes to talk to Marv himself?

"Are you threatening me, Ray?"

"I don't threaten, baby. I'm just suggesting."

"Are you *suggesting* if I don't come up with a million dollars you're going to tell Marv about us?"

"It don't need to come to that, baby," Ramon purrs. "I'm just sayin' a million bucks to Marv is chump change, *nada*. He'd give you that just to keep you happy."

"And if I say no?"

"You don't got to take a tone with me. I'm just sayin'."

"What are you *just saying,* Ray?" And she *is* taking a tone by now. "Because if you think you can blackmail me—*fuck* me—out of a million dollars by threatening to tell my husband about us, you are making a serious mistake."

And by now she's pretty much in his face, which Latin men don't generally tolerate very well, as evidenced by the fact that Ramon points an angry finger in *her* face and says, "You think you can fuck with me 'cause you some rich bitch married to a fuckin' billionaire? You think you can come sniffin' around me, take my classes, get in my pants, for nothin'? It don't work like that. Uh-uh. You play, you pay."

Linda gets out of bed, finds her thong panties on the floor, and steps into them. "You listen to me, Ramon," she says. "It was fun. You got greedy. It's over."

Ramon grabs the phone next to the bed and starts to dial. "How about I call Marv right now, huh, you cunt?"

Linda smacks him hard, and without hesitating, Ramon smacks her harder, which sends her backpedaling, almost losing her balance, and Ramon, his blood up now, and liking it, is all over her, grabbing a handful of her hair, ready to hit her again, when she grabs a gold-plated trophy resting on his mantel and clubs him as hard as she can, base first, just above the temple. A four-pound trophy with most of its weight in the business end will take the fight out of you pronto, and Ramon is no exception, staggering around crazily for a few moments before collapsing onto the bed.

CHAPTER 8

C HANGED INTO A FRESH T-SHIRT NOW, BOBBY HAS wandered out onto the deck overlooking the Hollywood Hills (did I mention you can see the HOLLYWOOD sign from there?).

When Bobby bought the house, the first thing he did was purchase a Bushnell XR90 electronic telescope. He told Vee it was for stargazing, and in fact, particularly on nights like tonight, you can see some pretty amazing close-ups of the moon, Venus, Saturn, and the Milky Way.

But the real reason Bobby paid almost four thousand bucks for Big Bushy (as he calls it) was so he could go out on the deck at night and spy on people. Get a look at Uranus, as it were. I know this because he told me. He said when he was a kid growing up in New York City, he loved to scan the neighborhood buildings with his father's binoculars, hoping to catch women undressing or couples fucking or whatever. He told me he once saw two guys doing the tango, nude. There was another guy he used to watch who'd screw his girlfriend in the morning, then lie around all day in bed jacking off to girlie magazines, then screw his girl again when she came home from work. He once even saw some guy looking at *him* through binoculars. But the absolutely coolest thing he ever saw was a guy making love to his pregnant wife on a mattress on the floor of their apartment bedroom. And the way the guy touched her, the sweetness of it, the tenderness with which he massaged her belly, was the sexiest thing he'd ever seen in his life. He said it wasn't so much seeing the sex that excited him but rather the feeling that he was somehow violating people's most private moments of intimacy without their knowledge.

I guess writers, by definition, are voyeurs. Bobby sure is, and on that hot night, alone, sick with jealousy and loneliness, he scans the houses in the canyon below, looking for something to distract him from the further contemplation of his totally fucked-up life.

And, boy, does he find it.

Through the telescope, Bobby spies every adolescent boy's wet dream: a man and a woman, really into it, fucking their brains out.

With the sliding glass bedroom doors open because of the heat, he can practically hear the sound of their bodies slamming into each other. As the telescope frames them in extreme close-up, Bobby can literally see the beads of sweat on their naked bodies, even though the house is a good thousand yards below and across the canyon.

Juicy.

The woman's lying on her back, her right arm partially obscuring her face, muffling her cries of passion, while the man is on his knees, upright between her thighs, his hands gripping her hips like the handles of a wheelbarrow, thrusting into and out of her, harder and harder, till both her arms go up over her head and she grabs the top of the headboard, bowing her pelvis up at him, her mouth wide with pleasure.

And right then, Jesus Christ, Bobby realizes he knows her. It's what's-her-name, she's married to Marv Paulson, a fat billionaire piece of shit who owns a bunch of television stations, and the young, well-built guy she's currently throwing a world-class hump into sure as hell ain't him.

Now Bobby sees the thing that changes his life. After Mrs. Marv Paulson finishes fucking this guy, their pillow talk begins to get a little less intimate and a little more animated, and before you know it, things are escalating to the point where they're up on their feet, bare-ass naked, arguing heatedly. Bobby can faintly hear the sound of their angry voices, but the words are lost as they reverberate through the canyon.

Finally, in a turn for the ugly, she hauls off and smacks him. Without hesitating, he smacks her back, push begets shove, and before you know it,

she picks up a trophy sitting on the guy's mantel
and whacks him over the head with it.

He staggers around for a few seconds like a
chicken with a wrung neck before collapsing, half
on, half off the bed. Even from a thousand yards
away, the guy looks dead.

As Bobby watches Marv Paulson's wife rush
around hurriedly throwing on her clothes, he suddenly remembers her name: Linda. And behind
that, in a rush, he also remembers her backstory,
which he knows because Vee was in some acting
class with her, and Linda told Vee her whole sordid
life history over a few too many margaritas one
night after class.

Linda Paulson's about forty years old, except for
her nose, which is around twenty-two, and her tits,
which are twelve. She grew up somewhere in Ohio,
a suburb of Cleveland, I think, and by the time she
was sixteen, she'd fucked the best-looking boys in
her high school (plus a couple of the teachers), she
knew she wanted to find fame and fortune (not necessarily in that order), and she figured, with her
looks, she had a shot at both of them in Hollywood.

After graduation, she hitchhiked to L.A. with a
friend, just for the summer, she told her mom. She
never came home. She got a job posing for underwear ads for the May Co., the kind you still see in
the *L.A. Times,* and used the money to finance acting lessons. When she started making the rounds of
casting directors, she caught the attention of one in
particular, who shall remain nameless, and happily

screwed him cross-eyed for a series of small roles in various television series. Off these parts, usually consisting of not much more than appearing in a nurse's uniform and uttering lines like "This way, Doctor," she got an agent, who told her he could make her a star if a) she fucked him and b) she got a nose job. She did both. He neglected to mention that her talent (at least for acting) was minimal, though, candidly, if that were a prerequisite for success, three quarters of the actresses working in television today would be unemployed.

Within eighteen months, Linda had gotten an agent, secured enough work in TV to buy a nice car, rented an apartment in a high-rise on Doheny between Sunset and Santa Monica, and expanded her network of friends and acquaintances to the point that her social life was pretty much a non-stop party. Of course, this was the early eighties, and cocaine was everywhere, which was how she wound up meeting her first husband, part of a group recreating in the guest bedroom of a house in Sunset Plaza doing lines of coke.

He was a fifty-six-year-old production executive at Warner Bros., and within a week she'd moved into his house in Beverly Hills. Within a year, they were married, and Linda was on her way. She stayed in the marriage for six years, hoping to parlay her husband's clout into a viable acting career, but it never happened.

Toward the end of the marriage, increasingly frustrated at her husband's inability to use his influence to her advantage, she met an incredibly good-looking young guy who was the brother of a girl she knew from acting class. He was visiting from Atlanta, the attraction was instant, and they wasted little time getting horizontal, and every other which way, with each other. Linda had always enjoyed (and been good at) sex, which was how she'd managed to tolerate the fifty-six-year-old tub of guts she married in the first place. But now, with a hard-bodied young man who told her he was a successful cable entrepreneur in Atlanta wanting to marry her, she dumped her husband in a heartbeat.

She married the sexy cable entrepreneur and moved back to Atlanta with him, figuring she was going to be the second coming of Scarlett O'Hara, only to discover the guy wasn't exactly what he'd said he was. He was in the cable business, all right, but the entrepreneur part was something of an exaggeration. What he actually did was drive a truck and lay cable for the local TV signal carrier.

Newly divorced, Linda returned to L.A. six months later and, with her last four thousand bucks, bought herself a spectacular pair of 36C's and dyed her hair blond. The rest, as they say, is history. Marv Paulson never stood a chance.

In his early fifties then, already forty pounds too heavy for his five-foot-nine-inch frame, Marv was a fat slob who stuck a napkin under his collar and sweated when he ate. He was also, at the time, closing in on a net worth somewhere in the neighborhood of 250 million bucks.

Among his other exotic tastes, Marv liked anal

intercourse. Linda was more than willing. He also liked to watch Linda make love to other women while he whipped his skippy. She was okay with that, too. Within a year of moving back to L.A., Linda was living large and opening mail addressed to Mrs. Marvin Paulson.

Believe me when I tell you that Linda's story is not that uncommon in Hollywood.

Hell, for that matter, neither is Marv's.

Marv is the kind of guy you love to hate. He started out life wealthy, thanks to a father who made millions building downtown office buildings in L.A. Marv cheated his way through high school, partied his way through college, knocked up a couple of girls along the way that his daddy paid to go away, and when the old man keeled over on the par-three fourth hole at Riviera one Sunday afternoon (he was six over par at the time), Marv suddenly had close to 10 million dollars of inherited wealth, which he shrewdly (not to mention shamelessly) leveraged into ownership of a few dozen flea-ridden flophouses. His timing couldn't have been better. Catching a wave of downtown real estate development, he sold off all the properties for ten times what he paid and put it all into television stations when they were a license to print money.

Then, when the good-time nineties finally rolled around and everybody and his cousin was getting rich in the stock market, Marv was getting even richer. Of course, this is where you'd hope a guy like Marv would've fallen flat on his ass, hanging around the market too long, watching his stakes in

Time Warner and Enron go belly up. Instead, like the creature he is, Marv got out of the stock market in March 2000, just before it began to nose-dive. While everyone else was buying more stock as the prices dropped, hoping to make a killing when the market turned north again, Marv was smugly saying things like "Trading down killed more Jews than Hitler."

So, while most of his cronies were getting their brains beat out in the market, Marv was buying himself a new Rolls-Royce, a Gulfstream 4SP, four floor seats to the Laker games, and a thirty-five-thousand-square-foot Bel Air mansion. It's safe to say, if there's ever a nuclear holocaust, Marv's the guy you want to be standing next to.

The problem is, when you're rich and you're wired up as nasty as Marv Paulson is, your perverse impulses tend to escalate, and Marv was no exception. I don't know what money buys you in Muncie, Indiana, but here in L.A., if you can imagine it, you can buy it, even if it's not exactly on page three of the Neiman Marcus Christmas catalog.

Over time, Marv's appetites grew to include pleasures as diverse as losing a million dollars at the craps tables in Vegas, then beating up black whores and taking a dump on them. Nice, huh?

My point being, at a minimum, you can begin to see how being married to a guy like Marv gets pretty old pretty fast if you're a sexy woman like Linda Paulson, and everywhere you go guys are checking you out, imagining soapy water running down your perfect 36C's, imagining what it'd be like if you were sucking *their* cock in the shower instead of fat Marv's. Jesus Christ, I'm getting a chubby thinking about it myself.

It's in that context you can pretty easily understand how come Linda likes to mess around a little on the side herself, just to keep her hand in, as it were.

And when it turns out this scumbag Ramon is trying to extort her by threatening to go public with their affair if she doesn't give him money, you can also understand why she'd whack him over the head with his proudest possession before she'd let him screw her out of the life she'd worked so hard to screw herself into . . .

CHAPTER 9

WHILE BOBBY WATCHES THROUGH HIS TELESCOPE, Linda wipes down the bedside table, the desk-top, and every other damn surface she thinks she might've touched in the last hour, before disappearing into the bathroom, reappearing moments later with her makeup kit in hand. Taking one last look around to satisfy herself that she's covered her tracks, she grabs her purse and exits the room, no longer in Bobby's view.

The writer part of Bobby's brain is screaming at her, *Come back, you dumb bitch. You forgot to wipe off the fucking murder weapon!*

And as if she's telepathically heard him, she reappears in the bedroom, grabs the trophy, wipes it cleaner than her husband wipes his ass with Tucks, and splits, this time for good.

A couple of minutes go by, or, for all Bobby

knows, maybe half an hour. Through the telescope, he can clearly see the guy isn't moving, or for that matter breathing, either.

"Holy shit," Bobby says out loud. "Holy shit."

He finally pulls back from the telescope, his head throbbing and his eyesight momentarily blurred from squinting through the eyepiece. His first thought as he moves back into the living room is to call 911, but halfway into dialing, a different thought occurs to him and he hangs up the phone.

What a great hook for a screenplay, Bobby thinks. Sort of like a contemporary *Rear Window.* A guy on his balcony, a down-and-out screenwriter spying on his neighbors through his telescope, happens upon a very sexy couple getting it on, and before you know it, they get in a beef, it gets violent, and she kills the guy with a statuette. And instead of calling the cops, the down-and-out screenwriter decides to insinuate himself into the lives of the principals so he can see how the story really unfolds, from the inside out, and then write the screenplay that'll resurrect his career.

With his brain racing and his head throbbing from too much adrenaline and an incipient hangover, Bobby quickly throws on a pair of jeans, a sweatshirt, and a pair of old sneakers.

In the kitchen now, he opens a cupboard under the sink and pulls out a box of latex gloves the maid uses when she's washing dishes. Grabbing a pair from the box, Bobby stuffs them in his pocket and goes through the laundry room to the garage, where he fires up the Boxster and drives down La Presa to the bottom of Outpost.

Parking well up the street, Bobby walks past seven or eight houses, carefully checking each one out, until he recognizes the dead guy's home. Pulling on the latex gloves, he checks to make sure the street is deserted before entering the property through the front gate. With his heart pounding louder than his sneakered feet, Bobby tiptoes along the narrow brick pathway running along the side of the house, almost jumping out of his shorts when the dog on the other side of the fence paralleling the pathway starts to bark furiously. Bobby freezes, terrified, and several moments go by before he realizes that either no one's home next door, they're home but they're deaf, or they don't give a shit that their dog is going berserk.

Bobby continues along the path until he reaches the back of the house and, finding the sliding glass door to the bedroom still open, lets himself in, relieved to hear that the dog has finally stopped barking.

Inside, wearing the gloves, careful not to disturb anything, Bobby closes the bedroom curtains before turning to face the room. He's probably written some version of what he's looking at a dozen times . . .

INT. BEDROOM — NIGHT
Through the open glass door overlooking the swimming pool, we see the victim, now nothing but a naked corpse, lying half on, half off the bed, head tilted at an odd angle, his cold, unblinking eyes staring vacantly into the camera. PAN DOWN *to the murder weapon, a four-pound gold-plated trophy,*

lying in plain sight on the floor next to the bed.
Bloodstains splatter the sheets of the unmade bed
where the victim's head rests, etc. etc. . . . .

The problem is, what Bobby's looking at now
isn't something he's written. It's the real deal, and
the real deal has him scared shitless, to the point
where he realizes how lazy and one-dimensional his
writing has always been.

For the first time in his life, he's suddenly conscious of the way in which real violence, with real
consequences, can turn the ordinarily orderly mind
into a screaming rat's nest of fear and confusion.
He's never even seen an actual dead body up close
(a murder victim, no less), let alone seen the murder
itself, and Bobby stands rooted to the floor, staring
at the corpse, trying to get his breathing under control, *willing* himself to calm down, to think clearly.

When he can finally hear more than just the
pounding of his own heart, Bobby cautiously approaches the dead body and stares down at it, afraid
to touch it, knowing it's dead, yet somehow terrified it'll suddenly move or groan or—God forbid—
grab his pant leg in some horrible death grip, the
torn piece of fabric becoming the fatal shred of
evidence that sends him, weak-kneed and loose-
boweled, to the gas chamber for a murder he didn't
commit.

"Get a hold of yourself, for Christ's sake,"
Bobby says aloud before finally checking to see if
the guy is dead, as if he didn't already know from

the color of his clammy, cold skin and his creepy, un-blinking eyes.

Eyeballing the room, Bobby sees a pair of pants lying nearby on the floor. Grabbing them and feeling around for a wallet, he reaches into the front left pocket and pulls out a small wad of cash, a couple of credit cards, and a California driver's license, all held together by two pink rubber bands. The driver's license identifies the deceased as one Ramon Montevideo, and now Bobby recalls why the guy's face seemed vaguely familiar to him. He was an actor in some Latino family drama that got canceled after thirteen episodes a couple of seasons back, and Bobby remembers this because Vee took a few acting workshops from him at a small theater in West L.A. last year and had nice things to say about him.

Bobby gingerly picks up the murder weapon, which, it turns out, is an acting award called an Alma, given by this Latino organization La Raza. The thing weighs a good four pounds, and it was probably lights-out for Ramon the second Linda whacked him with it. Think Barry Bonds jacking one into the bay beyond the right-field bleachers of Pac Bell stadium and you get the idea.

Now, as Bobby starts to relax a little, his story brain kicks in, big time. What had begun as this vague feeling that, in the midst of his own terrible failures, Lady Luck had chanced to present him with this incredible gift now begins to arrange itself into a coherent structure of events, each more dramatic than the last.

What could be more dramatic than the murder it-self, you ask? Well, for openers, how about this?

Bobby hears a sound from inside the armoire that faces the bed, kind of like the sound a VCR makes when the tape comes to an end and automatically rewinds itself. Opening the armoire's doors, Bobby finds, among other things, a tiny video camera that tapes, through a small hole drilled into the cabinet, Ramon having sex with (presumably) his various and sundry partners. And of course, where there's a camera, there's a recorder.

"Please, please, please," Bobby begs under his breath, hitting the EJECT button.

"Thank you, God," Bobby says as the cassette slides out.

If you've ever been to Las Vegas and pumped your last three bucks into a slot machine and watched as all four cherries come up in a row, you have some inkling as to the excitement Bobby is be-ginning to feel building inside him.

Pushing the tape back in, Bobby hits PLAY, then REWIND, and watches, thrilled, as the tape reveals, in absurdly comical backward sequence, first his own search of the bedroom, then Linda scurrying around cleaning up after herself, then the murder, then the argument with Ramon leading up to the murder, and finally the sex preceding their fight.

"Holy shit," Bobby says, actually grinning now as he pops the tape out of the machine again and sets it aside.

Under the shelf on which the VCR sits are three drawers, all filled with tapes, all numerically coded

and dated—the mother lode. Jesus Christ, Bobby
thinks, this guy must've fucked every woman in L.A.

Leaving the armoire for a moment, Bobby goes to
Ramon's desk and rifles the drawers. If I'm this guy,
he thinks, and I'm a big enough shitbird to secretly
videotape myself having sex with all these women,
I've also gotta have some sort of written catalog to
identify who's on which tape, right? I mean, when I
die and leave my library to the Museum of Television and Radio, I've got to give them the accompa-
nying paperwork.

And sure enough, in the back of the top right-
hand desk drawer, under a bunch of loose papers,
Bobby finds what he'd hoped for, Ramon's "little
black book" with the names of all the women he's
fucked, the corresponding dates and numbers that
identify their various tapes, plus one-word com-
mentaries and grades on their sexual talents: Anal.
Oral. Moaner. Screamer. Doggie. Orgasms. Letter
grades from F to A-plus. Bobby can't help wondering, Does this asshole send out report cards?

Bobby thumbs through the book quickly, hoping
to find names of women he knows, never thinking—although in retrospect, God knows why not—
that among the dozens of women's names would be
his own wife's, along with the date, September 18,
2002, and this notation: Screamer. Oral. B+.

Stunned and angry, Bobby's not sure who he's
madder at—Vee, for screwing this guy practically
under his nose, or Ramon, for being enough of a
prick to actually give her a fucking grade (literally).
Vee winds up winning by default, seeing as how

Ramon's already dead, which doesn't change the fact that Bobby'd still like to give this dead asshole a swift kick in the head. And suddenly, out of God knows where, an image of Marv Paulson taking a crap on Ramon's chest makes Bobby laugh out loud. The only difference between him and Marv, Bobby realizes (aside from about half a billion dollars and eighty pounds), is that if Marv knew his wife had been banging Ramon, he probably would've wanted to watch.

Bobby returns his attention to the armoire where all the sex videos are neatly stacked and labeled with initials, and he scans the collection, looking for the one of his wife blowing this dead prick. Removing that tape from the collection, Bobby adds it to his little care package, which now consists of the sex-and-murder tape, Ramon's little black book, and the tape of his wife and Ramon fucking. Grabbing them up, Bobby takes one last look around, then lets himself out of the room the way he came in.

Moving swiftly back along the narrow pathway that parallels the side of the house, with the dog starting to bark again on the other side of the fence, Bobby exits to the street through the little gate, his heart pounding again, like it's going to explode out of his chest.

Scanning the street, satisfied he hasn't been seen, Bobby hurries up the street, gets into his Boxster, hangs a U-turn, and hauls ass back to his own house.

S AFELY HOME, BOBBY GOES INTO THE KITCHEN, POPS
the cork out of a bottle of wine, and pours a
glassful, which he proceeds to chug down like
you'd chug a bottle of beer at a frat party. A second
glass likewise chugged finally gets his nerves under
control and, third full glass in hand, Bobby goes
into his little office to fire up the TV and VCR.

Sitting on his desk is Ramon's little black book,
along with the two videocassettes—the one with
the murder on it and the other with his wife on it.
Sick as he knows it'll make him to see it, he figures
he better get it over with. He slips the tape into the
VCR, hits PLAY, and there on the small screen is his
wife, Vee, flat on her back, her legs wrapped
around Ramon's torso, hanging on for dear life, the
whole time screaming, "Fuck me, oh yeah fuck
me," in Ramon's ear, then rolling him over and slid-

ing down between his legs to give him a hummer for dessert.

Bobby bolts from behind his desk, barely making it into the little guest bathroom off the entryway, where he pukes his guts out into the toilet for the second time tonight. It's the story of Bobby's life these days that the only thing he can do twice in one night anymore is puke.

Cleaning his mouth off with a towel, he breathes deeply, trying to get his emotions under control before going back into his office, where, blessedly, the tape of Ramon and his wife has run out.

Popping the tape out of the machine, Bobby slides in the one of Linda Paulson banging Ramon, giving as good as she gets, nothing romantic here, just balls-to-the-wall hot sex, artlessly, lovelessly performed by two people who couldn't give a rat's ass about seeing to each other's emotional needs.

Bobby wonders what compels a guy to secretly tape himself having sex with all these women. Does he watch afterward and get off on it all over again? Or is it more about getting off on the sick power of knowing these women are on *Candid*-fucking-*Camera*?

When it comes to men, Bobby thinks, Linda Paulson's got her taste in her kidneys. But then, *après* sex as it were, there it is—the argument that escalates from push to shove to Linda caving in Ramon's skull with his own award trophy. Watching it again in the safety of his own little office gives Bobby a feeling of deep satisfaction, knowing that at least this prick won't ever fuck another guy's wife again.

As the wave of jealous rage engulfing him finally begins to recede, Bobby thinks, Christ, what have I done? And his writer's voice answers immediately: *For openers, you've seen a murder committed by someone you know, which makes you a material witness. You've also entered the victim's home and stolen evidence, which not only makes you a thief but could get you indicted for breaking and entering, obstruction of justice, and being an accessory after the fact to murder.*

Realistically, Bobby assures himself, none of this will happen unless he was seen entering or leaving Ramon's house, which he's positive he wasn't, or unless he loses his cool, which he's equally positive won't happen. But shit happens. Everybody knows that. Bobby's written a hundred scripts about a hundred arrogant assholes who never thought they'd get caught, and they were.

Call the cops now, he tells himself. Tell them what you saw, tell them what you did, give them the tape, you're a hero, a Good Samaritan who witnessed a crime and phoned it in. No charges, lots of good ink, you'll dine out on it for years.

But then he reminds himself of the starlet who tells Mike Ovitz she wants to blow him and Ovitz saying, Okay, but what's in it for me?

And the answer is, Nothing, numb nuts. There's nothing in it at all except a lifetime of regret that you didn't grab the brass ring when you could have, because you chickened out.

And then, finally, there's this: in a weird way, Bobby feels as if what he saw tonight is the exact break he's been waiting for, better even than Ed McMahon showing up at his door with a check for ten million bucks and telling him he's won the Publishers Clearing House sweepstakes.

Thusly inspired, Bobby stashes the tapes and the black book in the back of his desk drawer and boots up his computer. He's got a screenplay to write and, goddamnit, he's gonna write it.

Clicking into his Final Draft program, he settles in front of the computer and types onto the blank screen:

FADE IN.

CHAPTER 11

THE NEXT MORNING, SOMEWHERE AROUND TEN o'clock, an actress friend of Ramon's comes by his house, probably thinking she's going to get laid, and instead finds more of Ramon stiff than she'd bargained for and calls the cops.

Detective Dennis Farentino catches the case. A homicide veteran, Dennis is very cool—someone you can't help being drawn to, unless you're a shitbird, in which case he's your worst nightmare. Dennis will tell you he never started a fight in his life, but by the same token he never backed down from one, either. What he won't tell you, unless you ask, is that he never lost a fight, which is pretty amazing when you figure that, by his own estimate, he's had maybe a couple of hundred.

Dennis was a superior high school athlete but a lousy student, so after graduation he went into the military, did six years, then came out and joined up again, this time with the LAPD. He was a natural cop: smart, coolheaded, brave, with an uncomplicated respect for authority. Within four years, he made detective, first with Narcotics, then Robbery Homicide.

Women, on the other hand, were a different story. Dennis never had a clue. Not that it stopped him, or them, from getting together. It was the *staying* together that caused him problems. I'm no shrink, so I won't bother to give you my twenty-five-cent analysis of why Dennis fucked up two marriages. I suspect it has to do with the fact that Dennis is threatened by the smart women and has no patience with the stupid ones, which narrows the field considerably.

I guess smart women give Dennis problems because he can't compete with them verbally in an argument. He holds his own when the argument is in his head (usually after the fact), but when it's actually happening, his anger tongue-ties him, and in the heat of battle, rather than get abusive (he never hit a woman in his life), he just shuts down emotionally. Relationship-wise, that's what they call non-productive.

Notwithstanding, because he's a handsome guy, in a quiet, understated way, and because a lot of women are attracted to the withholding type of guy, Dennis makes out like a bandit. Women always think they can get him to open up, which he certainly takes advantage of, but then when it comes to the heavy lifting real relationships require, they discover, to their dismay, that Dennis fatigues easily.

To his credit, I guess, in spite of the two busted marriages and a whole bunch of romances that went nowhere, you won't find a woman Dennis has ever spent time with (including the ex-wives) who doesn't have nice things to say about him.

Dennis has been divorced three or four years, there's no woman currently in his life in a serious way, and he probably drinks more than is good for him. He works his ass off staying fit, on the theory that if you're going to abuse yourself, you gotta be in shape for it. And he is. Dennis doesn't look like the kind of guy who's afraid to get physical.

So the way it is with Dennis these days is, he's got a small number of women friends he'll occasionally sleep with when they're between relationships, plus whatever comes his way in the natural course of things, as long as he doesn't have to work too hard for it.

Fourteen years on the job, Dennis has always kept his nose clean, at least professionally speaking. He's the kind of guy people always underestimate, which, according to him, is a good thing. He calls it his Columbo act. He wants everyone to think they're smarter than he is, because arrogance will fuck you up, every single time. (I happen to think that's true of our business, too.)

If asked, Dennis will describe himself as someone who's okay knowing he'll never be more than what he is—a cop who's seen too many stiffs and fucked too many women (I didn't know you *could* fuck too many women, but I'm not as cool as Dennis is, plus I'm married, which I take pretty seriously, most of the time at least).

Anyway, it isn't long before Ramon's house is a cordoned-off crime scene, swarming with uniformed cops, detectives, crime-scene investigators, and—as always—hovering around and above the perimeter, the media, already sensing this could be a good one. A fairly well known Latino actor found naked and bludgeoned to death in his bedroom isn't exactly your garden-variety homicide.

To the untrained eye, a crime scene is a pretty chaotic environment. But everybody present has a specific job—photographing the scene, dusting for prints, collecting evidence. You're looking for cigarette butts, chewed gum, used tissues, hair, any kind of DNA material you can compare against a suspect's, when and if you make an arrest.

It doesn't take a genius to figure out that the Alma award is the likely murder weapon, so it's bagged and tagged, along with the used condom fished out of the toilet that didn't go all the way down when it was flushed. You don't see the good-looking babe on *CSI* doing *that,* I'll bet.

Dennis also tells his partner, a beefy older guy named Lonnie Rosen, to dump the phone for the numbers of whoever Ramon called or called him. Download his cell phone, too.

Then, out by the pool, Dennis questions the girl who found Ramon's body. She's young, maybe twenty-two or twenty-three, she's already got her starter set of implants, plus the requisite nose job, and she tells Dennis she's a student of Ramon's and that her name is Lisa Ratner.

Dennis wants to tell her that as long as she's changed every other damn part of herself, she may as well get rid of the *Rat* in her last name, but instead he asks, "What kind of student?"

"An *acting* student," Lisa says, in a tone implying Dennis must be some kind of an idiot.

"I guess I should've figured, someone as pretty as you," Dennis says. "Where does he teach?"

"At the West Side Theater Arts School, on Pico Boulevard."

"How long have you and Ramon been romantically involved?" Dennis asks.

"We're not," she says, offended.

It always amazes Dennis that people lie to him about stuff like that. "So then you came over to his house because . . ."

"I came over because he invited me to, so we could talk about a scene I did in class the other night."

"Oh yeah? What was the scene?"

"It was from *After the Fall*."

"Arthur Miller," Dennis says. "I always liked that play. I'd've liked to see what you did with it."

"Thank you," Lisa says.

"Okay, so you came over and what—rang the doorbell?"

"Yes." And now her eyes start to puddle up.

"And when there was no answer," Dennis prompts, "you went around the side of the house and let yourself into the bedroom through the sliding glass door?"

"It was open," Lisa says, and bursts into tears. "I'm, like, I can't believe it. It was horrible. I've never seen a dead person before."

Dennis puts a comforting arm around her and tells her he knows how awful it must've been and that it's okay if she doesn't want to stick around. He can always find her later if he needs to ask anything else.

By now, Lonnie's discovered the fuck tapes in the armoire and sends a uniformed officer to fetch Dennis.

Inside the bedroom, Lonnie says, "Take a look at this," and hits the PLAY button on the VCR. Suddenly, there's Ramon, lying on the bed, hands behind his head, cool as you like, watching his dick get sucked by a woman with big, hard breasts, her ass smiling at the camera while her head bobs up and down. "This douche bag must have over two hundred tapes of this stuff," Lonnie says.

"Was that in the machine or did you just put it in?"

Lonnie says the machine was empty, but between Ramon being bare-ass naked and the half-flushed condom they recovered in the toilet, you've got to assume that whoever he was banging killed him and took the tape.

"Well," says Dennis, thumbing through the drawers full of tapes, "there's a couple hundred suspects right here, plus you gotta assume a jealous husband or boyfriend's in the picture somewhere."

Lonnie says, "It's a dirty job, partner, but we're gonna have to look at all of 'em."

Dennis hasn't seen Lonnie this animated in a long

time. Big, overweight, in his late forties, and twenty-three years into an excessive affection for gin martinis, Lonnie's the kind of guy who makes lunch dates at eleven-thirty in the morning just so he can get that first martini in him on an empty stomach. After eighteen years in Robbery Homicide, he's witnessed enough crime scenes that he sleeps every night of his life with his gun under his pillow, which thrills Mrs. Rosen no end. ("That's the only goddamn gun in this bedroom that works," she says to Lonnie about once a month.)

Around noon, Ramon's maid, Esperanza, shows up and immediately goes hysterical when she finds out Mr. Ramon *es muerte*. Dennis calls over a uniformed cop named Suarez to act as a translator. "Ask Esperanza was she here yesterday," and when Suarez translates the question, she bursts into fresh tears, and Dennis can't understand a word of what she's saying. Finally, Suarez tells him that Esperanza is afraid Dennis thinks she killed Ramon, and Dennis says to the cop, "Ask her was she here last night?"

More excited Spanish, then Suarez tells Dennis she was home with her family last night.

"Okay, tell her she's not a suspect. I just want to know if she has any idea who might've come over last night. Did he have a steady girlfriend? Can she give us any names of women he'd been seeing recently?"

More tears, lots of talk, lots of head shaking, and Dennis gets the drift that Esperanza is a dead-end street, information-wise, though she does confirm a portrait of Ramon pretty much in sync with the murder scene itself, telling Dennis, through Suarez, that Ramon had different women to the house all the time. She knows this because she had to change the sheets every day, for obvious reasons, and she was always cleaning up Ramon's disgusting litter, which she's too embarrassed to get specific about but which Dennis takes to mean everything from stray items of women's underwear to used condoms. Esperanza tells Suarez she never saw any of these women, since her hours are noon to five every day, and in fact hardly ever saw Ramon, either, since he was usually at work.

Off the canvass of the neighbors, Ramon is variously described as sexy, friendly, charming, and in one case an asshole—this from a guy who lives across the street, who accuses Ramon of having made a pass at his wife, telling Dennis he's not surprised someone popped him.

"Should I be looking at *you* for murder?" Dennis asks this guy, with a straight face, and the guy is immediately defensive, telling Dennis he was at the Dodger game last night—he's got the stubs to prove it.

There's a general consensus among the neighbors that women came and went at all hours, but as far as last night is concerned, no one can volunteer having seen anyone who may have been visiting Ramon between the hours of nine and eleven P.M., roughly the time of death as determined by the M.E.

CHAPTER 1 2

LATER THAT AFTERNOON, DENNIS GOES OVER TO THE West Side Theater Arts School on Pico Boulevard, where Ramon taught, and meets the owner of the place, an old queen named Lars, who is stunned at the news of Ramon's murder. He keeps patting his heart and saying, "This can't be happening. I just do not believe this."

But of course, his disbelief notwithstanding, Ramon *is* a murder victim, Lars *is* a drama queen, and Dennis *is* a ruggedly handsome and extremely sexy cop. So, pale blue eyes glistening with tears, Lars volunteers that Ramon was one of his *most* sought after teachers, and not just by the females. He was a favorite with men, too.

"Was Ramon bisexual?" Dennis asks.

"Oh, would that he was," Lars says. "But that wasn't his movie. What I meant was, he had a macho thing about him that men responded to, and he knew how to communicate from his gut."

Lars tells Dennis that Ramon's classes, Tuesday and Thursday nights from eight to ten, were always full, and there was always a list of actors wanting to get in.

"Was Ramon having an affair with any of his students in particular that you knew of?"

"Oh my dear," Lars says, pressing his fingertips into his chest. "Ramon was not exactly what you'd call a monogamous creature. That wasn't his movie, either. Ramon played the field, and as you can tell from the size of his classes, he had a very large field to play in."

"What about beefs? Any conflicts between his students over Ramon's affections?"

Lars tells Dennis it was no secret that Ramon was a player, but he was so open about it, so charming and seductive, that no one was under any illusion Ramon could be tamed. "And, of course, women talk, don't they, so it's no secret that, among other things, Ramon supposedly had a member *formidable*."

Deadpan, Dennis tells Lars that he saw Ramon's dead body and even on the mush, it looked like Ramon probably went a good eight, nine inches.

"Oh my," Lars says, patting his heart.

Dennis wonders, would Lars be kind enough to furnish a list of all Ramon's students?

"Of course," Lars says. "Anything I can do to help. In fact, if you'd like, Detective, I can give you their head shots as well, if you promise to return them when you're done."

Head shots are eight-by-ten-inch glossy photos actors give to producers and casting directors, with their résumés on the back, and having them will allow Dennis and Lonnie to look at Ramon's sex tapes and match names to faces (and asses, one presumes).

Dennis gratefully takes the list and photos, thanks Lars for his cooperation, and tells him if he thinks of anything at all that might be useful, don't hesitate to call. Lars accepts Dennis's card and says, with a flirtatious little smile, that he might call even if he can't think of anything useful.

In the detectives' squad room of the Hollywood Division, Dennis and Lonnie plow (you should pardon the expression) through boxes full of Ramon's Funniest Home Videos, using the list Lars provided to identify most of the women on the tapes. And it doesn't surprise Dennis in the least that one of the first tapes they look at stars—who else?—Lisa Ratner.

About thirty tapes later, Lonnie shakes his head admiringly. "Jesus, is this a great country or what? People always think cops get a lot of trim, but this guy, Christ, it's like a license to steal."

But for Dennis, it's just depressing. The sex isn't sexy, the endless coupling seems joyless, and in the sheer volume of it, maybe Dennis is seeing something uncomfortably reminiscent of his own journeyman's sex life.

Dennis and Lonnie split up the names of all the actresses on the list Lars provided and commence interviewing them. The ones of particular interest to Dennis are the ones that *don't* match up with any of the sex tapes, on the theory that if Ramon was killed by the last woman he fucked, she probably would've taken the tape.

Lonnie likes to bust Dennis's balls by pointing out the flaw in the theory: if they were secret tapes, how would she know they existed at all?

"Fuck you," says Dennis. "At least I *got* a theory. All you got is a jealous hard-on watching this prick get sucked and fucked by half the actresses in Hollywood."

Anyway, off Dennis's theory, such as it is, he winds up calling Linda Paulson, wondering could they maybe get together to talk about Ramon.

Linda says she doubts she'll be of much help, but she'll be delighted to meet with him. "Would you like to interview me down at the jail," she asks, "or would you prefer to come up to the house for a cup of coffee?"

Dennis says the house would be better, as the screams from all the suspects being beaten up by the cops "down at the jail" might be off-putting.

Linda laughs. "I like you already, Detective," and they make an appointment for later in the day.

CHAPTER 13

DENNIS HAS SEEN A LOT OF WEALTHY PEOPLE'S HOMES, but even by the standards of wealth he's familiar with, the Paulson estate stands alone. On three acres of prime Bel Air real estate, the two-story, thirty-thousand-square-foot house is beautifully situated on the highest point on the property, which also features a guest house, a tennis court, a pool, and separate servants' quarters.

Dennis drives through the tall iron gate and tins the armed private security guy in the blue blazer, who calls him sir and directs him up the driveway to the front of the house. At the door, Dennis quickly huffs into his cupped palm to make sure the garlic from the linguini he had at lunch hasn't hung around past its welcome.

The door opens, and a uniformed maid greets

Dennis and walks him into the library, telling him Mrs. Paulson will join him shortly.

Looking around, Dennis is prepared to bet his pension no one living here has ever read a single one of the leather-bound volumes lining the walls of the magnificent wood-paneled room.

"I've read every one of them," Linda Paulson says, entering the room, her hand outstretched in greeting, as if she could also read minds. Then, smiling, she says, "*Not.*"

"What a place," Dennis says, shaking her hand, and he's not kidding.

"It's bigger than we need, but it was my husband's before we were married," and her self-deprecating little shrug says, what's a girl to do?

Dennis tells Linda he appreciates her taking the time to see him, he won't keep her long, but if he could just ask her a couple of questions, he's interviewing everyone who knew Ramon, he'll let her get back to her reading.

His little play off her joke earns him a dazzling smile, and Dennis thinks to himself he wouldn't mind seeing a tape of Linda Paulson banging *any*one.

"I doubt I can tell you much about him past what you probably have already," Linda says. "I hardly got to know him at all."

"How long were you taking his class?" Dennis asks.

"About four months or so. I used to be a working actress in my salad days, before I met Marv, and while I haven't really pursued my career since then,

DEATH BY HOLLYWOOD 77

I thought it would be fun to take some classes, kind of stretch out my acting muscles."

She tells Dennis she certainly knew Ramon was something of a womanizer, and while it was none of her business, it was pretty obvious that he'd slept with a number of the girls in his class.

"Did he ever come on to you?" Dennis asks, and Linda laughs.

"No," she says. "I don't think he was very interested. I'm a happily married woman, Detective, and there were a lot of very pretty single girls in class who were half my age."

Dennis is willing to bet double or nothing that Ramon *was* very interested, that he was probably all *over* Linda Paulson. What he isn't sure of is whether *she* was all over *him,* though from having seen pictures of her fat slob husband, Marv, Dennis figures it's at least fifty-fifty she thought about it.

Dennis has been around long enough to understand why a beautiful woman like Linda Paulson would hook up with a fat piece of shit like Marv, if you don't think about it too specifically. If you only think about the fact that, okay, he's rich, they hang out with lots of celebrities, they have floor seats at the Laker games, there's a certain cachet in Hollywood that comes from being with a rich, powerful tub like Marv—Dennis gets it. But stop and think about it *specifically.* What's it like being with this fat fuck when you're *not* out in public at Spago or sitting in your floor seats at the Laker game or sitting next to Jay Leno in Marvin Davis's tented backyard at a table for ten that your fat-ass husband paid fifty thousand bucks for?

Or how about what's it like watching him shovel forkfuls of pasta into his mouth or listening to his wet, disgusting farts when he's brushing his teeth and doesn't think you can hear it over the sound of the water running?

What's it specifically like having to spread your legs for this pig first thing in the morning, pretending you love it, while he airmails his disgusting wake-up breath all over you and you're covering your mouth with the pillow so he'll think you're trying to stifle your cries of ecstasy when all you're really trying to do is get your nose out of the jet stream?

Start thinking about it like that, Dennis says to himself, it's a whole different picture, and he can't help wondering what kind of woman is willing to whore herself out to a guy like that for money. Does that sound naïve? Maybe in this town it is. Maybe in any town. But still.

So anyway, Dennis does his Columbo shit, admiring the museum-quality art on the walls, telling her he hopes she wasn't offended by his questions, he's just doing his job, etcetera etcetera. And then, as she's walking him to the front door, Dennis says, "It probably won't come up, but if it did for some reason, could you verify your whereabouts the night Ramon was murdered?"

"Am I a suspect, Detective?" Linda asks coyly. "Should I lawyer up, as they say?"

Dennis grins. "You're watching too many cop shows on television."

"You're right about that. Marv had his poker cronies over," Linda says, "and I stayed up in my bedroom watching television. Pretty romantic, huh?"

In spite of himself, Dennis is charmed. "Let me ask you one last thing, Mrs. Paulson—if you hardly even knew this guy, how come you called him on the phone the night he was murdered?"

To which Linda replies, slick as snot on a doorknob (Dennis's expression, not mine), that the reason she called was, she was looking for a recommendation from him about who she should partner with on a scene for class.

"Oh yeah?" Dennis says. "What was the scene?"

"Well, I'm probably a little old for the part by now, but I wanted to do Maggie from *Cat on a Hot Tin Roof.*"

"Good choice," Dennis says. "People say Williams is dated, but I always loved that play."

CHAPTER 14

ONE OF THE ACTRESSES IN DENNIS'S PILE OF EIGHT-BY-tens from Lars is a terrific-looking blonde named Veronica Wallace, and even though she's not a charter member of the Ramon Montevideo Secret Sex Tape Club, there's something about her photo that he's drawn to. Maybe it's her genuine smile or her sparkling eyes, which, you can tell, even in a black-and-white picture, are blue.

He places a call to the agency listed on her résumé, the Artists' Group, and winds up speaking with some fast-talking little jerk named Ari Goldstein. Dennis says he's trying to get in touch with Veronica Wallace, and the kid says, "In reference to what?"

Dennis says her name came up in a murder investigation, and Dennis needs to talk to her at her earliest convenience.

"Holy cow," Ari Goldstein says. "Is she a suspect?"

"Just tell her I'd appreciate a call back," Dennis says, and he gives Ari his cell phone number.

Dennis figures that actresses are always available for calls from their agents, so he isn't surprised when Veronica Wallace calls him within thirty minutes. The words *murder investigation* in connection with your name will usually get your immediate attention.

Over the phone, Dennis says he has a list of Ramon's students and he's interviewing everyone on it. Could he meet with her for a few minutes at her convenience?

"Sure," Veronica says, "but I don't know how much help I'll be. I didn't know him except to take his class."

Dennis assures her that's okay, he's just going down the list, talking to everyone, regardless. "You never know how sometimes a casual observation, or something you don't even think is all that important, can really make a difference."

So Veronica tells him she's got an audition at Paramount. She can swing by after, say between three-thirty and four?

"That'd be great," Dennis says, and because he knows that talking to cops makes most people nervous, he tries to relax her by asking what she's auditioning for, and she tells him she's going up for a role in *JAG*. "I bet you'd look great in one of those uniforms," he says, and with just that one remark he can almost feel her relax.

She laughs and says, "Let's hope the producers feel the same way."

After Dennis hangs up the phone, he stares at her picture for a good long time, knowing you can never tell much about a person from a photograph (unless, of course, it's of a dead body) but deciding nevertheless that Veronica Wallace doesn't look the type who could kill a man in hand-to-hand combat.

When Veronica finally shows up, looking around the place with the kind of nervous curiosity you always see in people who've never been inside a police station before, Dennis says to himself, *Wow*. Because while you can always hope that the rest of the package measures up to the head shot, more often than not, it doesn't. Sometimes, in person, the actress is much older. Or heavier. Or the body's not so good. Maybe her legs are upside down—thin in the thighs and thick through the ankles—which is a particular turnoff for Dennis. But Veronica Wallace in person delivers on the promise of her picture. Great face, great eyes, great body, and when she smiles—*wow*. Even when she says the line he's heard a hundred times before—"I've never been in a police station before"—she says it in a way that makes him realize he's starting to get a crush on her.

"We could've done this someplace else," he says.

"No, I wanted to see it."

"Well, the Hollywood Division of the LAPD isn't being featured in *Architectural Digest* anytime soon."

Her laugh is a compliment, and it fills him with warmth. "Can I buy you a cup of coffee?" he asks.

"No thanks."

"C'mon, let's go in here," and Dennis ushers her into the little TV room, where he and Lonnie have been watching all of Ramon's tapes. "I appreciate you coming in," Dennis says.

"It's my pleasure, Detective."

"Call me Dennis, please."

"Thank you."

"Do you mind if I call you Veronica?"

"My father's the only one who ever called me Veronica," she says. "Everyone else calls me Vee."

Dennis and Vee sit down on the couch facing the TV set, and he likes the way she doesn't seem to mind that it's a ratty piece of shit. "I see what you mean about *Architectural Digest*," she says, but there's no put-down in her tone.

"How'd your audition go?" Dennis asks.

"Okay, I think, but you never really know till your agent calls. I was always so insecure. If the producer was nice, I'd think I did great, and if he was a dick, I'd think I did lousy. Now I just wait till the phone rings."

Vee winds up telling Dennis a couple of her worst audition stories, including the time her husband set her up to audition for a movie he'd written, and he was so nervous introducing her to the director that when it was time to leave the office, he opened the door and backed into the guy's private bathroom.

"Did you get the part?" Dennis asks.

Vee shakes her head. "I was so embarrassed, I could barely get through the audition. I never read for anything my husband wrote again."

"So you're married."

"Separated. In fact, we split up the same day Ramon was murdered." Which is the signal Dennis was waiting for to commence his interrogation.

"How well did you know him? Ramon, I mean."

Vee says she only knew him professionally, but he was a really good teacher and a charming guy.

"He ever make a pass at you?"

Vee laughs. "Ramon made a pass at everyone. You'd be insulted if he didn't."

"But you didn't respond."

"No."

"Do you know anyone who did?"

"Other than myself, I'm not sure I know anyone who didn't."

"Do you know Linda Paulson?"

"Sure."

"What about her?"

"And Ramon?"

"Uh-huh."

"I don't know. Y'know, she's older, very attractive, but she's married to a very rich guy . . . If I had to take a guess . . ." Vee shrugs. "I don't know . . ."

"What was it that made Ramon so attractive to women?"

"You always knew what the deal was with him. He always made you feel sexy, and he was totally clear it was just about sex, not about getting involved, and that's very appealing to a lot of women."

"But not to you."

"I guess I'm not that kind of girl," Vee says, and

Dennis is rewarded with a smile when he remarks that he's glad she isn't.

"Did any of the women in your class talk about their relationship with Ramon, tell you any stories about him?"

"What kind of stories?"

"That he was kinky for this or that, or he liked it rough?"

Vee shakes her head. "No, nothing like that. But sometimes they'd gossip about what a stud he was." And she holds her hands about a foot apart to indicate the rumored size of Ramon's dick.

Dennis grins, which tells Vee, among other things, that he's not afflicted with penis envy. "Any jealousy you picked up on, or maybe a jealous husband or boyfriend you heard about?"

"I'm sorry, no."

"Did he have any enemies that you knew of?"

Vee laughs, then says no.

"What's so funny?"

"I'm sorry, but it's like I'm reading for a part in *Law and Order* or something, except it's for real."

"Y'know, it's none of my business," Dennis says, "but I spoke to your agent, this Ari Goldstein guy, and he sounded kind of like an immature jerk."

Vee laughs again. "Ari Goldstein *is* an immature jerk. And he's not my agent. He's my agent's assistant."

Now it's Dennis who laughs. "Gee, I guess he lied to me."

"There's a shock," Vee says.

An awkward silence then, as if there are no other questions to ask, but neither of them wants the conversation to end. Finally Dennis stands, signaling the interview's over. "Thanks for coming in, Vee."

"My pleasure," she says.

"I know this isn't strictly speaking professional of me, but would you consider going out with me sometime?"

Vee's smile lights him up. "I've never gone out with a policeman."

"You don't have to worry," Dennis says. "I'm potty-trained."

"That's a relief," Vee says.

Out in the squad room, Dennis asks for Vee's phone number, and she writes it for him on the back of her eight-by-ten. "I'm staying with a girlfriend in Hollywood till I figure out my life," she says, "but that's my cell number."

And then, because Dennis can't ever stop thinking like a cop, or maybe it's because he already has feelings for Vee that are making him nervous, he asks her if she ever heard about Ramon liking to tape himself having sex with women.

Vee looks almost shocked by the question. "No, I never heard that. Did he?"

"Not to my knowledge," says Dennis.

"What a creepy thought," Vee says, and then she blesses him with her smile again. "Call me." And she's gone.

CHAPTER 15

PERSONALLY, I'M NOT A BIG FAN OF MOVIE PREMIERES, or for that matter the gigantic parties that follow. For one thing, they can cost anywhere up to a million dollars, which is an insane amount of money to add to the already horribly bloated bottom line of most big-budget movies. Also, you can't even really justify the cost as part of your publicity-and-promotion campaign. The premiere itself, with all the fans, the TV cameras, the klieg lights, the paparazzi, provides the media bounce. The party after is nothing more than a self-congratulatory jerkoff. And finally, there's the simple stupidity of it. Let's face it—paying a million dollars for a party is like paying a thousand bucks for a bottle of wine in a restaurant. It may be a showy gesture, but no matter how good it is, six hours later it's still piss.

Or maybe I'm just cynical. The fact is, people in

and aspiring to *be* in the industry love these parties. It's an opportunity to network on someone else's dime. It's an opportunity to hook up. It's a chance to amortize the cost of your new tits. And of course, like all industry functions, it's a chance to aggrandize yourself—i.e., to lie. I mean, how else are you supposed to get good at something if you can't practice?

I'm telling you this because I happened to attend, albeit reluctantly, the premiere of the latest Tom Hanks movie, as well as the party immediately following, in a giant tent set up a block away from the movie theater in Westwood. I was there because I represent one of the six credited writers on the movie, Bobby Newman, which is how I can tell you the next part of the story with the certainty that it's true.

But before I get to that, you're probably wondering what Bobby and I were doing together after I fired him. What happened was, a couple of days after Ramon was murdered, Bobby called me to apologize. He said he realized what a terrible pain in the ass he'd become, how he'd taken Vee's love and my friendship and support for granted, and how his drinking had pretty much killed his marriage, not to mention shut off his creative faucet. He went on to say that maybe Vee leaving and me firing him back to back was just the wake-up call he needed to get his shit together and that, finally, he was back on track. He said he was going to do everything possible to show Vee he was a changed man and that he was hoping she'd be willing to give him another chance. He also told me he'd have the Brian Grazer draft finished by the end of the week. He'd literally been working on it night and day, plus— for the first time in years—he'd gotten an idea for an original screenplay, which he thought was absolute dynamite.

When I asked him what it was about, he told me he wasn't talking; that when he talked, he didn't write, and he wasn't going to dissipate his creative focus by discussing it, even with me.

Say what you want. I've known this guy a long time, and one thing I know for sure is when he's bullshitting me and when he's not, and I heard in his voice that he's not. So I unfired him, and to tell you the truth, I'm glad. I was having second thoughts about what I'd done anyway. Not so much because I thought I was wrong, but because my timing was lousy. Here was a guy whose career was going down the tube, his wife had dumped him, and I fired him the same day.

In retrospect, I've come to believe I was piling on, so when Bobby called me sounding so genuinely optimistic about himself, I was more than happy to let us both off the hook, which is how I came to be his date at the party after the premiere of the Tom Hanks movie, which Bobby really had done some first-rate work on.

So Bobby and I are standing in line waiting to get a drink at one of the bars when he spots Linda Paulson in the company of her husband, Marv. "Linda," Bobby shouts over the din.

She sees Bobby and smiles, not because she recog-

nizes him—she doesn't—and not necessarily because Bobby's a good-looking guy, though he is.
She smiles because when you're wandering around
a two-acre tent filled with a thousand milling people (the stars, producers, director, and studio exec-
utives all have reserved seating; the rest of us
basically suck hind tit) and you look like Linda
Paulson (spectacular) and you're holding the fat,
sweaty hand of a guy who looks like Marv (porcine),
any potential distraction is worth an exploratory
smile.

Dragging Marv over, she gives Bobby a big "Hi"
and a kiss on the cheek, and Bobby—no stranger to
the intricacies of introducing yourself to someone
you don't know or who doesn't know you—says,
"You look great," and immediately sticks his hand
out to Marv.

"Hi, Marv, Bobby Newman. I wrote this movie.
Our wives took an acting class together."

Brilliant. Think about it. For openers, he's telling
her his name without acknowledging she didn't
know it in the first place ("Hi, Marv, Bobby Newman"). But he's also identifying himself as someone
with legitimate credentials, with enough stature to
warrant talking to ("I wrote this movie"). Then he
disarms her husband's natural suspicion of any
man his wife smiles at by identifying himself as a
married man whose only claim to a casual acquain-
tance with Linda is through his own wife ("Our
wives took an acting class together"). The particular
brilliance of that gambit is that Marv instantly loses
interest in Bobby, and by the time he's introduced

me to both of them, old Marv's looking around for someone more interesting to talk to.

Spotting a poker crony in the company of two prostitutes, Marv tells Linda to stay in line and get him a drink. "Nice to meet ya, fellas," and he's gone, a fat, white predator heading into deeper waters, with no natural enemies in sight.

"How's your wife?" Linda asks, having no idea who she's asking about.

"Vee? She's great," Bobby says, and now Linda has a name with which to recollect a face.

"Is she here?"

Bobby says, "I haven't seen her, but if she is, it's not with me." Which is the last piece of the puzzle artfully presented, letting Linda know that Bobby's a player.

Within two minutes, I've become about as useful to this conversation as tits on a bull.

"I really liked the movie," Linda says by way of complimenting Bobby on his work. "I know I should know, but what other movies have you written?"

Bobby scrolls his credits, which are numerous and impressive, and Linda knows they're legit as well, because if they weren't, Bobby wouldn't be running them for her in front of his agent.

Next thing, Bobby says, "Isn't it tragic about Ramon?" and Linda manages to get a little wet-eyed, telling Bobby how stunned and saddened she was when she heard the news. Bobby asks if she's spoken to the cops yet, and she allows as she has, given they're interviewing anyone who ever took his class.

"They've probably talked to your wife, too."

"If they have, I wouldn't know it," Bobby says. "In fact, Vee left me the day Ramon was murdered." In other words, telling her he's alone but he didn't dump Vee; she dumped him.

"What a grim coincidence," Linda says, and by now we're at the bar, Bobby's ordering Chardonnay for both of them, and I'm getting a light beer to go with the cold shoulder.

"What about Marv?" Bobby asks, referencing the drinks, and Linda says Marv'll take care of himself. And with both of them now in orbit around the twin stars of Ramon's murder and Bobby's busted marriage, Bobby needs only to take care of one more piece of business before docking maneuvers can commence. "I know a lot of the homicide detectives from Hollywood Division. Who's in charge of the case?"

"I don't know if he's in charge," Linda says, "but I was interviewed by a Detective Farentino."

"How's it going, did he say?" Bobby asks. "Anybody they're looking at?"

"I don't think so. At least I didn't get that impression."

"Did you know most homicides solve within forty-eight hours or they don't solve at all?"

"Really?" And now Bobby's telling her about all the cop movies he's written and the project he's currently working on, which he'd actually love to talk to Linda about sometime, being as there's a role in it she'd be perfect for. Docking is now imminent, and actual coupling can't be far off.

"Maybe we could meet for coffee or something. I'll tell you all about it," Bobby offers.

"I usually have lunch at the Ivy on Robertson," Linda says, "if you'd like to get together tomorrow."

Bobby says that'd be great, he's been craving their chicken tostada.

"It's a done deal then," she says, shaking both our hands. And with a disarming smile she tells us she'd better go find Marv before he dumps her for a younger broad.

We watch her depart in search of Marv, looking every bit as good from the rear as from the front. "For a guy who desperately misses his wife, that was awesome," I tell Bobby, and I mean it.

CHAPTER 16

M Y WIFE AND I HAVE ALWAYS TRIED TO TEACH OUR kids that if they don't lie, they'll never have to remember what they said. The problem is, every kid's a natural-born liar. Excluding the occasional child who turns out to be a sociopath, I guess the good news is that most of them lie because they know the difference between right and wrong, and they're so frightened of being punished that when they inevitably do wrong things, it's easier to lie than face the consequence of their misdeeds. The irony, of course, is that the consequence of lying is almost always worse than the consequence of the original sin, and the ability (or inability) of parents to teach that lesson to their children is the differ-ence, finally, between happy and unhappy kids. And if you think there's a tougher job for parents than that, either you don't have children or you don't think lying is that big a deal. Unfortunately, in Hollywood the latter is probably truer than the former, which is why raising kids in this town is such a bitch.

I tell you this only to provide some context for Bobby's lunch with Linda at the Ivy on Robertson, a meeting freighted with lies—and their first cousin, secrets.

Linda's secret is she killed Ramon. Bobby's secret is he knows it. And almost always, at some point, secrets mutate into lies, and lies kill.

The Ivy on Robertson is a bright, crowded room with lots of tables, lots of linen, uncomfortable, quaint wooden chairs, and too many fat, cushy pillows, which slide all over the place when you try to settle into them. That said, it's an enormously popular eatery and a particular lunchtime favorite of women like Linda Paulson, who have a ton of money and an abundance of time, all cooing and clucking and air-kissing one another.

Just as you'll see the alpha-male elite powering up at the Grill, you'll see their wives and girlfriends in their parallel universe at the Ivy. And if you think there's any less power or influence on display there than at the Grill, think again. In this crowd, with the notable exception of Linda Paulson, the murder weapon of choice is the cell phone, and you can hear them ringing, chiming, and buzzing all over the room.

Linda is sitting at one of the best tables, all the way back in the left-hand corner, and when she sees Bobby enter, she smiles and waves him over.

It's one thing to look great and sexy at night in a dimly lit party tent where everyone's half-bagged. It's another thing to pull it off at high noon in the brightness of the Ivy on Robertson, and Linda Paulson does it effortlessly.

Notwithstanding Bobby's secret agenda in wanting to get to know her, she's the first woman Bobby's met since Vee left that he finds himself sexually attracted to. In part because there's good chemistry between them, but more important, because of the videotape—the one sitting in the back of his desk drawer—showing her, like a female predator, fucking her prey, then killing him. It's not the sex or even the violence so much as his secret knowledge of it, and secret knowledge is the intoxicating essence of voyeurism.

Over iced tea and salad for Linda and a chicken tostada for Bobby, the two of them sniff around each other, bullshitting and flattering each other. Obviously, Bobby's trying to get into her head, because if you're writing a movie about a woman with the balls to kill her shitbird lover, you want to have a pretty good idea of who she is and what drives her.

Bobby would love to ask her why she married a slob like Marv Paulson. He'd love to ask her why, with her looks and her money, if she's going to fuck around on Marv (and who wouldn't), why it would be with a scummer like Ramon. Maybe her taste just runs to men who treat her like shit.

For her part, Linda finds Bobby more interesting than most men she meets, because he seems to be more interested in what's on her mind than under her shirt.

Bobby grills her about her background as an actress, telling her he remembers her work. He also tells her that time has blessed her, that what was pretty a dozen years ago has matured into genuine beauty. Linda figures Bobby's blowing smoke up her ass, but she likes it. The irony is, among all the other lies, Bobby's telling her the truth on this one. Plastic surgery aside, Linda's got one of those faces that really do mature beautifully, and she's taken good enough care of herself that, at forty, she looks better than she did at thirty, and thirty was pretty goddamn good to begin with.

Finally, Bobby works his way around to asking Linda if she's heard anything more about Ramon's murder case.

"Not really," she says, "but I got the impression from the detective who interviewed me that they don't really have a whole lot to go on, kind of like a fishing expedition, and the fish aren't biting."

Which gives Bobby, who's written so many cop-themed scripts, a chance to trot out his writer's expertise, suggesting that in a case like this, the cops might have a lot more than they're letting on.

"Like what?" Linda asks.

"This is pure speculation on my part," Bobby says, "but you've got your good-looking, semi–well-known Latin-lover type, single, an actor, a teacher, a stud, plus I read in the paper he's done time for rape assault, which probably none of the women in his present life knew about. So if I'm a cop, I want to look at who he's sleeping with. Maybe there's a jealous husband or boyfriend, or maybe, based on his past, he's got a violent streak in him and when he gets too rough with whoever he was having sex with, she kills him in fear for her life."

"Is that your theory of the crime?"

"I don't have one," Bobby says. "But if I'm writing the movie, it's a better story if he's killed by a jealous husband or boyfriend than it is if it's just, say, some junkie break-in, Ramon struggles with the guy, the guy kills him, and the girl Ramon was in bed with flees."

"If that's the case, why doesn't the girl come forward?"

Bobby shrugs. "Maybe she's married, she's got too much to lose." And then, unable to resist the opportunity, he asks, "If it was you, for instance, would you go to the cops?"

"I see your point," Linda says, and then, with a wicked smile, adds, "How about this? Ramon's having a three-way—which, believe me, if you knew Ramon, isn't that far-fetched—things get a little out of hand, and one or both of them kill him."

"That's good," Bobby says. "I didn't think of that. You oughta call the detective and run it by him."

"I don't think the detective needs a bunch of amateur sleuths pestering him with their theories of the crime."

"I guess not," Bobby says, "but it's fun to speculate."

By now, they've graduated to a nice bottle of Ferrari Carano Chardonnay, and Bobby changes the subject to how long she's been married, does she miss acting, what are her hobbies, that kind of shit.

Linda gives him the Classics Illustrated version of her life, the PG edition, if you will, and in turn, Bobby tells her the story of his breakup with Vee. He confesses how self-absorbed he was, how he drank too much, wasn't sensitive enough to his wife's career needs, with the result being he was a lousy husband who screwed up his marriage—a mistake that, if he ever gets another chance, he'll never make again.

No shrinking violet when it comes to letting men know how she feels about them, and emboldened by their newfound emotional intimacy, Linda reaches across the table and puts her hand on Bobby's wrist. "You know what I find very sexy?"

"What?"

"Honesty. I can't remember the last time I met a man as honest about himself as you are," she says.

And if Bobby weren't thinking he's on the verge of getting laid, he would probably laugh out loud. Instead, he just drops his eyes and goes with a simple, heartfelt "Thank you."

Another reason Linda's attracted to Bobby is that he's not sexually aggressive. He's letting her lead, she senses, because he instinctively understands she's a destination resort and that even if the journey takes a while, it'll have been worth the trip.

"I don't want to embarrass you," she says quietly, "and I'll understand if you think I'm going too fast, but is there someplace we can go?"

Which is how they find themselves, twenty minutes later, on the deck of Bobby's house, barefoot, overlooking the canyon, with her looking through Bobby's telescope and Bobby telling her he'd love her to come up some night and watch the stars with him.

Turning away from the telescope, Linda slides into his embrace, and they kiss for the first time, tenderly, patiently, as if she has no idea that Ramon's house is a thousand yards below them in the canyon. "You have soft lips," she says, and kisses him again.

Bobby takes her hand and leads her to his bedroom, and they make love. Having had the benefit of watching her bang Ramon as if they were both going to the chair at midnight, Bobby goes the other way, slow and gentle, in no particular rush to get them there but enjoying the rush when they do . . .

CHAPTER 17

MOST CASES ARE SOLVED EITHER BECAUSE SOMEONE rats out the perpetrator or because the perpetrator commits another crime for which he's finally caught, and winds up going for the five others he did. And then there's the fact that most of the time, criminals wind up making a mistake that gets their asses nailed to the wall. As Dennis is fond of saying, "Thank God they're stupid."

The problem with this case, so far as Dennis can tell, is that whoever killed Ramon wasn't stupid. Angry, yes—stupid, no. Dennis is pretty convinced that Ramon was killed either by the woman he was fucking or by some other woman he *wasn't* fucking, who was jealous of the one he was, or by a husband or boyfriend of same. Dennis is inclined to discount the husband/boyfriend theory off the crime scene itself, on the assumption that if Ramon had been killed by a man, there would've been more signs of a struggle. Which only leaves a couple of hundred women this guy fucked over the last year or two as potential suspects.

Between them, he and Lonnie have interviewed maybe a third of the women on the tapes and maybe another dozen more who'd been in Ramon's class but, at least going by their absence from the tape library, hadn't fucked him.

There were fingerprints all over the house and all over the bedroom—Ramon's, the maid's, maybe ten other women's, but none of them looks good for the murder. And since there were no prints at all on the murder weapon, Dennis assumes the assailant had enough presence of mind to clean up after herself.

The phone dumps haven't given them anything much, there aren't any witnesses who saw anyone coming or going the night of the murder, and two hundred suspects are as bad as no suspects at all.

Comparing notes with Lonnie almost a week into the investigation, Dennis realizes that basically they're nowhere. It may be too soon to throw up his hands in surrender, but Dennis knows the drill. Fresh murders take precedence over cold ones, what's on the front page on day one gets buried on page sixteen of the Metro section on day five, and in another week, for all practical purposes, the case is deader than the proverbial doornail. And it's during Dennis's morose meditation on the stalled progress of the case that Bobby Newman calls.

Bobby introduces himself as a screenwriter who's

currently writing a script about a murder investigation, telling Dennis he got his name from Linda Paulson, who had nice things to say about Dennis after being interviewed by him regarding Ramon Montevideo's murder.

This is Hollywood, so Dennis is not unaccustomed to the occasional phone call from writers looking for technical advice, and since he recognizes several movies that this guy says he wrote, Dennis agrees to meet him for dinner that night at the Palm, on Santa Monica Boulevard.

Dennis can't stand watching movies and TV shows about cops, because the writers don't generally give a shit about authenticity, so when he does get a chance to help one of these guys out, he usually does it. Besides, they always pick up the tab, they eat up his stories along with their prime rib, and there's always the off chance you can actually wind up making some dough as a technical adviser.

That night, Bobby gets to the Palm about ten minutes early and orders a Tanqueray martini straight up, with extra olives. He's on his second one by the time Dennis arrives, and Bobby recognizes him instantly by the way he carries himself and by the way he scans the patrons at the bar. Bobby half shouts, "Dennis?" over the din in the room and waves him over.

Bobby likes Dennis instantly. He doesn't seem to have that defensive attitude that a lot of cops he's met over the years have, particularly in L.A. In that regard, he reminds Bobby more of some of the New

York detectives he's met—friendly, talkative, with an easy sense of humor.

Dennis orders a Jack Daniel's on the rocks, and while he's waiting for the drink, he asks Bobby what is it exactly he's working on that requires his technical expertise, or does he just want to know what most writers want to know?

"Which is what?" Bobby asks.

"How to get away with murder," Dennis says deadpan, using his forefinger to swirl the ice cubes in the Jack Daniel's the bartender puts in front of him.

"Every successful writer I know gets away with murder every time he sits down at his computer," Bobby says, and Dennis graces him with half a smile. "Actually, if I had the balls to commit a murder, I probably *would* ask."

"Truth is," says Dennis, "anyone's capable of murder under the right circumstances." And just like that, they're talking about Bobby's favorite subject these days.

"So you know Linda Paulson," Dennis says, and Bobby tells him he doesn't know her very well, but they wound up having a chat at the premiere party for the new Tom Hanks movie, which he worked on, by the way, and the subject got around to Ramon Montevideo's murder and the coincidence of both her and Bobby's wife having taken his class.

Arguably, Hollywood's filled with more gold diggers than any other city in the world, Bobby observes, but at least Marv Paulson got his money's worth when he hooked up with Linda. Bobby says he's got to respect the fact that she's stayed with him over the years in spite of the fact that everybody in town knows what a sleaze Marv is. "You married?" Bobby asks.

Dennis says no, he's been divorced for years and isn't sure he'll ever get hitched again. "You said you were married to an actress."

"Currently separated," Bobby tells him, "but I'm hoping we can maybe work it out and get back together. Actually, I'm surprised you haven't interviewed her yet."

"What's her name?"

"Vee."

"Wallace?"

"Yeah, that's her professional name."

"I did interview her," Dennis admits, "but I didn't know she was your wife. She seems like a nice girl. I hope you work it out."

A sudden image of Vee going down on Ramon flashes across Bobby's mind, and he actively banishes it—something he couldn't have done a couple of weeks ago. Practice makes perfect, he thinks, then tells Dennis it's a tough town to stay married in given all the career conflicts people in the entertainment business have, but even so, he's hoping they can figure things out.

Dennis says it's not the easiest thing in the world being married to a cop, either. Cops work odd hours. They interface with strange people. They're susceptible to corrupting influences. It's tough on relationships, especially when the cop blows off steam by going out drinking with his co-workers, not unlike a billion other guys after a long, hard day on the job. The problem is, those billion other guys don't have a gun on their hip and a badge in their pocket. A cop who's metabolizing a six-pack and gets cut off on the freeway by some idiot in a pickup can put a very different spin on the notion of road rage.

By now they're in a booth, Dennis is on his third Jack Daniel's, and Bobby's halfway into a bottle of Paul Hobbs Chardonnay. Bobby asks Dennis how the case is going, if Dennis doesn't mind his asking.

Dennis says it's a tough case—Ramon was a big-time womanizer—and in a situation like that, you're looking at a lot of suspects. You've got to in-terview every one of the women, their jealous boyfriends or husbands, neighbors, friends—it takes fucking forever, and you don't even know if you're going in the right direction.

"For all I know," Dennis says, "it could've been a simple break-in, some junkie looking for a quick score, and maybe the woman Ramon was fucking is taking a leak in the bathroom or she's in the kitchen getting a bottle of water, she hears the com-motion, and hides out till it quiets down. And then, after the junkie kills Ramon and flees the scene, she splits too, and doesn't come forward, because she shouldn't have been there in the first place."

"See, I never would've thought of that," Bobby says.

Flattered, and embarrassed that he is, Dennis changes the subject, asking Bobby again what he's working on.

Bobby tells him he's developing a kind of *L.A.*

Confidential type of television series for HBO. "Basically, I'm a movie guy," he tells Dennis, "but HBO's almost as good. *Sopranos, Sex in the City, Six Feet Under.* I figure if Alan Ball can do TV, so can I."

"Who's Alan Ball?" Dennis asks innocently, and Bobby grins, not sure if Dennis is making fun of him, but thinking that if he is, he's good at it.

By the time dinner's over, Bobby and Dennis have hit it off, talking about their respective careers and the seemingly natural Hollywood intersection of cops and writers. Dennis shares some of his better cases with Bobby, and Bobby flatters Dennis again by telling him he's got a natural sense of story, suggesting maybe they could work on the HBO thing together. Dennis would supply the raw material, Bobby would do the writing, and together they'd make some real dough, like that New York cop did on *NYPD Blue.*

Outside, after Bobby's paid the tab and shmeared the weasel and while they're waiting for their cars, he invites Dennis to come up to the house one afternoon on one of his days off, maybe shoot the shit when they're not too loaded to remember what they talked about.

Dennis says that'd be great, and as Bobby gets into his car, he says that if he gets pulled over by the cops for DUI, he's going to tell them it's Dennis's fault.

And that's dinner.

CHAPTER 18

I'M ALWAYS AMAZED HOW SECRETS, LIES, AND GENERAL bullshit never seem to get in the way of mutual interests, or even friendship for that matter. Take Dennis and Bobby. Dennis has a serious crush on Bobby's wife, Bobby knows who killed Ramon Montevideo, and neither man has any intention of confiding in the other. Nevertheless, they're instinctively drawn to each other, which is why, on a warm Saturday afternoon, Dennis drives up to Bobby's house, where, over a couple of Coronas on the deck in back of Bobby's house overlooking the canyon, they dig into each other's lives a little, and Dennis confesses that he's always wished he could write.

"Anyone can write," Bobby says. "You're a cop, you've got great stories, you know how to tell 'em. And if you can tell a story, you can write a story."

"I don't know," Dennis says. "Every time I ever tried to write, my brain would freeze up."

"Which is why we should be working together," Bobby says. "You tell 'em to me, I'll write 'em."

Which gets Dennis to grilling Bobby about writing in general, as in how do you get your ideas, how do you develop them, do you come up with characters first, or stories, how does it work?

Bobby says that sometimes it starts with a character, sometimes it's a situation or a story notion, occasionally it's something of a thematic nature, but that whenever he gets an idea, he dumps it into his computer and leaves it there to cook. He tells Dennis it's like meeting an interesting woman for the first time. "I always wait a week to see if I'm still thinking about her before I call. That way, I know I'm not wasting my time. It's the same with an idea. If I'm still thinking about it a week later, I know it's worth developing."

"Of all the stuff you've ever written," Dennis says, "what's your favorite?"

"Seriously?" Bobby asks. "Ever?"

"Sure."

"You're going to laugh, but my favorite piece of writing ever is a short story I wrote about five years ago that I've always wanted to turn into a novel or a film but never got around to."

"What's it about?"

"It's basically about a talking dog."

Dennis does laugh. "Are you kidding? Like a kids' movie?"

"Kind of," Bobby says. "But I think adults would like it, too."

"I'd like to read it."

"I've never shown it to anyone."

"Why not?"

"It's not the kind of stuff anyone would take seriously."

"How do you know if you've never shown it to anyone?"

"If you're serious, I'll print out a copy for you. You can read it the next time you're taking a crap."

And while the printer is exhaling pages, Bobby opens another couple of beers and takes them out onto the deck, handing one to Dennis. "What about you?" he says. "Do you like being a cop?"

"Yeah, actually, I do."

"What is it you like? The danger? The romance? The adrenaline rush of going through doors?"

"I hate going through doors," Dennis says. "I hate the violence."

"Then why did you become a cop?"

"I guess because I wanted to help people, and I accepted that violence was a part of it."

Bobby confesses that he's always been afraid of violence, and Dennis points out that people who are afraid of violence usually live longer.

"I've never had a fight in my life," Bobby admits.

"If you really had to, if your life was on the line, or the life of someone you loved, trust me, you'd fight."

"I don't know if I'm brave enough."

"Fighting isn't about bravery," Dennis says. "It's

about failure. Failure to communicate, failure to compromise, failure to say 'I'm sorry.' "

"How many fights have you had?" Bobby asks.

Dennis smiles ruefully. "Let's just say I've had my share of failures."

And back and forth it goes, both men being uncharacteristically intimate, enjoying the surprise of new friendship.

Over a third bottle of beer, Bobby tells Dennis his HBO pitch, which is basically a contemporary version of *L.A. Confidential*. Having written about cops as much as he has, Bobby's take on them in general, and the LAPD specifically, isn't that far off the mark. The problem is, as Dennis sees it, there's nothing particularly fresh about it. Denzel Washington played a rogue narcotics detective in *Training Day;* there's this cue ball named Michael Chiklis who plays a similar-type asshole in *The Shield*. But does anyone really need to see yet another show depicting the LAPD as a bunch of immoral, fascist boneheads who kill, brutalize, and trample citizens' rights under color of authority?

"Are you saying it doesn't happen?" Bobby asks. "That certain cops don't keep a cold gun handy just in case they need to kill somebody off the books? Or that Rafael Perez *didn't* shoot those gangbangers or steal all that dope and plant all those weapons or lie like a fucking rug under oath to secure dozens of wrong convictions?"

"I'm not saying it doesn't happen," Dennis says. "All I'm saying is, there's over eight thousand cops in L.A., and suddenly it's all about the few rotten apples instead of the vast majority of good, hard-working cops who bust their asses trying to make L.A. a better, safer place to live."

"People *want* to see Denzel being a badass or Chiklis putting his gun in some guy's ear. That's the shit they love."

"Well, at least you admit it's shit," Dennis says.

"Okay," says Bobby. "I'm Chris Albrecht at HBO and I come to you looking for a fresh take on cops. I tell you I'm open to anything as long as I'm not seeing it everyplace else. What do *you* pitch me?"

"I don't know," Dennis says. "I never thought about it."

"Think about it now. How do you put old wine in a new bottle so people *think* they're getting something new, which is what they always *say* they want, but you're actually giving them something familiar, which is what they *really* want."

Dennis gets up, goes to the railing, and looks down into the canyon. "You know what my favorite realistic cop show of all time is? The one that made me want to be a cop in the first place?"

"I don't know," Bobby answers. *"Dragnet?"*

"Uh-uh. *Columbo.*"

"You said realistic."

"It was realistic."

"Come on," Bobby scoffs. "A shabby cop with a glass eye, all he ever wears is that stupid raincoat, going up against all these arrogant, smart-mouth killers, always pretending he's an idiot"—and here, Bobby goes into a pretty decent Peter Falk imitation—"Oh by the way, y'know, I got a cousin, and his wife's sister's daughter says blah blah blah, and y'know this old dried-up piece of chewing gum I scraped off the bottom of the chair in your private screening room? It's got *your* fingerprint smack in the middle of it, from when you wadded it up and stuck it under there, and when I test it for DNA, it's going to prove *you* killed your gorgeous, two-timing wife with that frozen leg of lamb."

And by now Bobby's got Dennis laughing, shaking his head, saying, "No, no, you're missing the point. Sure, the *show's* unrealistic, but the *character* isn't. Columbo was a real *detective*. He *solved* crimes. He caught bad guys. And he didn't do it with his fists or his gun, he did it with his *brain,* which is what really good police work should be. He always made the bad guy think he was smarter, that he could fuck with Columbo's head, and then Columbo'd lull the guy into revealing some clue or other, and little by little, piece by piece, he'd put the puzzle together and get the guy, because the guy was too fucking arrogant to see how smart Columbo really was. Shit, it's thirty fucking years, the guy's gotta be over seventy years old by now, and they're still making *Columbo* movies."

"Your point being," Bobby prods.

"My point being, forget about your old-wine-in-a-new-bottle shit. It's about *great* wine in any bottle, because great wine just keeps getting better with age."

"So you're saying what? Go to HBO with a fucking thirty-year-old *mystery* show? I can see them right now, leaping out their forty-second-floor office windows with excitement."

"Bust my balls all you want," Dennis says. "I'm just telling you, as a cop, what gets me going."

And out there on the deck, going back and forth at each other, having fun with it, Dennis starts screwing around with Big Bushy, swinging it left and right, trying to focus on various points of interest in the canyon below. "Look at that," Dennis says, like Christopher Columbus discovering America. "You can see Ramon Montevideo's house from up here."

Seeing the opening he's been looking for, Bobby says, "So okay, suppose you're Columbo. How do you think your way through *that* case?"

So Dennis takes him through it, leaving out a lot of the specifics, but in general terms telling Bobby that in a case where there are so many suspects, you try not to form too many opinions too early.

"You interview all the women he's screwed, you consider the possibility there's a jealous boyfriend or husband in the picture, or that maybe it was a simple break-in gone bad. Basically, I'm just trying to get a handle on the case, but I'm spinning my wheels. By this time, most cops would be getting frustrated, or bored, and would move on to other things. But not Columbo. Columbo knows that if someone's gotten away with murder, or knows something about someone who's gotten away with murder, either they're eaten up with guilt or they're bursting with pride, and one way or the other, they want to talk about it. So if I'm Columbo, I hang around, I keep talking to people, and finally, what happens? Suddenly this screenwriter guy, completely out of the blue, calls and says he's looking for help with a project, could he buy me dinner and pick my brain. And as it turns out, he's married to one of the actresses in Ramon's class, and on top of that, their marriage went south right around the time Ramon got whacked. So now I'm up at this writer's house, and what do you know? He's got this big-ass telescope, and when you look through it from the deck of his house, you can see Ramon's place. You're practically on top of it."

And now it's Bobby laughing. "See? I was right. You would make a good writer, 'cause you think that way."

On a roll now, enjoying the warmth of Bobby's undivided attention, Dennis says, "So I think to myself, maybe this guy's looking through his telescope one night, the wife's supposed to be at her acting class, but instead, he sees her banging this guy Ramon so close up you can see the pimples on his ass, and in a jealous rage, he goes down to Ramon's house to confront him. One thing leads to another, push comes to shove, and the writer clocks him over the head and kills him, like that movie where Richard Gere kills this French asshole his wife's banging."

"*Unfaithful.*"

"Yeah, that's the one."

This guy is good, Bobby thinks, then says, maybe with a little more sarcasm than he intends, "Now all you gotta do, *Lieutenant,* is find the piece of

chewing gum with my perfectly preserved fingerprint on it and you've got me dead to rights."

"Nah," Dennis says. "You didn't kill this guy. I'm
just saying, though, that's how you learn to think—
that's how Columbo thinks—one thing leading to
another, and before you know it, you've caught a
break."

Disregarding the age-old cautionary "If it ain't
broke, don't fix it," or maybe it's the one that goes
"Let sleeping dogs lie," Bobby says, almost like he's
offended that Dennis dismissed him from suspicion
so easily, "How can you be so sure I didn't do it?"

"Because it was a crime of violence," Dennis explains, "and you told me you're afraid of violence."

"I *am* afraid of violence, but if this guy's screwing
my wife, maybe I'm so angry and jealous, my natural timidity gives way to my need for revenge."

"Except there were no signs of a struggle, which
you'd expect if Ramon had been killed by a jealous
husband."

"I don't know," Bobby says. "You confront a guy
in bed with your wife, you hit him a quick shot over
the head with his own Alma, that'll take the struggle right out of him."

"Uh-uh," Dennis says. "You may be a lot of
things, but a murderer isn't one of 'em."

What he doesn't say, of course, is that Bobby's
just given him his first break, since it's not public
knowledge that Ramon was killed with his own
Alma. Which means either Bobby's a mind reader
or he's in shit up to his hips. And the strong *eau de
pee-yew* suddenly wafting up the canyon on the

wings of a late summer breeze leads Dennis to suspect the latter.

Which reminds me of this joke about the guy who
dies and goes to hell. The Devil welcomes him and
shows him three doors, telling him that behind
each door is a different vision of hell and he's got to
choose one of them to spend the rest of eternity in.
The Devil opens the first door, and the guy sees a
vast ice floe, with half-frozen people, blue and shiv-
ering with cold, dressed in nothing but loincloths,
picking away futiley at the glacierlike ice with tiny
little hammers. The guy says to the Devil, "Don't
make me go in there. I can't stand the cold. I moved
down to Miami just to avoid New York winters."

The Devil says, "No problem," and opens the
second door, behind which are countless naked,
sweating people, blistered and bleeding, shoveling
molten rock out of a volcanic sea of hot, bubbling
lava. The guy gasps. "Shut the door—it's horrible. I
once took a helicopter tour of the volcanoes in
Hawaii and had a panic attack. I can't catch my
breath just thinking about it."

Now the Devil opens the last door, revealing a
vast crowd of men, as far as the eye can see, all
standing in shit up to their knees, drinking coffee.
"Now, this doesn't look so bad," the guy says, relieved. "I could see spending eternity in here."

The Devil says, "You'd better be sure, because
once you go in, it's forever, and forever means that
when you've been dead *a hundred million years,*
you'll have just *begun* to be dead."

The guy says, "No problem. I'll take door three,"

and he wades in. Someone hands him a cup of coffee, he's standing there in shit thinking, This isn't so bad, when a booming Voice comes over the loudspeakers: "All right, you guys, coffee break's over. Back on your heads!"

I mention the joke because under the circumstances, it's hard not to imagine Bobby Newman wading into a sea of shit up to his knees, thinking, This isn't so bad, only to discover, after it's too late, that it was just a coffee break.

CHAPTER 19

MONDAY MORNING, DENNIS GETS TO WORK EARLY AND
fires up a pot of coffee. Pouring himself a cup,
he settles in at his desk to read the story Bobby gave
him. It's called "First Dog," and this is it . . .

*You're probably not going to believe this. I don't
know that I would, either. Sometimes I'm not sure I
believe it even now. But it's true, even though I'm
not going to swear on my mother's eyes or anything
stupid like that. You can judge for yourself after I
tell you the whole story.*

*My name is Ron Barkin, which might be vaguely
familiar to you even if you can't exactly place
where you heard of me. I'm the creator and executive producer of the hit television show* Sleeper.
*We're in our fourth season, we've won three Best
Show Emmys, and in addition, I've personally*

earned two Emmys for Best Dramatic Writing—one for the pilot episode and another for the season opener of year two.

If you're one of the nine or so people in America who don't own a TV set, Sleeper is about this college professor at a small Eastern campus who teaches English Lit. He's a genius—a brilliant professor, loved by his students, admired by his colleagues, tolerated by the administration—an amazing scholar, gifted in his ability to communicate, educate, and entertain, all in one package. His classes are always SRO. Complicating matters is the fact that the professor is a drunk and a degenerate gambler who, when loaded, becomes profoundly rude and antisocial, whether shooting out the lights of a squad car, losing a month's salary at the racetrack, or mooning the wife of the university president at a faculty-student tea. His escapades are legend, and only lend to the general aura of notoriety that surrounds him.

A slob who lives most of the time in his office, he has a habit of disappearing for several days on end, only to reappear hollow-eyed, unshaven, and rumpled—the classic post-binge, hangdog, guilt-ridden drunk, always forgiven by his students and colleagues because he's so brilliant, mesmerizing, charming, and self-effacing. In short, he's a lovable, bad-boy genius rogue.

Except here's the catch: it's an act. The professor's not a drunk at all, or a degenerate gambler, or an all-around world-class fuckup. What the professor really is, is a sleeper—a deep-cover CIA opera-

tive, like the Scarlet Pimpernel, who's called in peri-odically (like, say, once a week) to deal with (i.e., eliminate or neutralize) various domestic terror threats, be they Middle Eastern, American (à la Timothy McVeigh), or organized crime.

That's the basic idea.

Anyway, six years ago, I wasn't exactly a house-hold name. I was a writer with a lousy marriage and a lousy job, working on a TV series I hated. I wasn't exactly phoning it in (the marriage or the job), but I had no passion for either.

I was in my middle forties, plugging along, out of shape and putting on weight, when I got a call from my mother in New York telling me my father had dropped dead on the sidewalk from a heart attack.

When I got back from the funeral, I did some quick math on my life and didn't like the bottom line. I'd been married for twenty-three years, and it had never been an easy marriage. Think about try-ing to squeeze a square peg into a round hole and you have the idea. There were career ups and downs (both of us), weight ups and downs (hers, and they were mostly ups), there were anger issues (mutual), libido issues (more hers than mine, until the last couple of years), struggles with depression (also hers), and enough money spent on marriage counseling to fund a small third-world nation.

Finally, after our kids were pretty much grown and gone, the marriage went from strained to stale to stagnant, and I figured if I didn't do something about it right away, I never would. Truth is, scared as I was to change my life, I was so unhappy I *thought if I didn't leave, I'd die. Literally. My blood pressure was going through the roof, I was having anxiety attacks, and when I finally went to this shrink a friend of mine recommended, I spilled my guts. I said, "I'm forty-six, I've been married half my fucking life, my kids are grown, I feel like shit, and life is too short to stay miserable any longer." So this shrink says to me, "If life was short you wouldn't be here. Life is* long." *Which hit me like a ton of bricks.*

Life is long.

So five days later, I moved out. I rented a dark, damp, termite-ridden house in Mandeville Canyon and commenced my new life.

There was this woman I'd been friendly with for some time who was an independent producer at Paramount, where I worked. We hit it off almost immediately, and I would be lying if I told you I didn't have the occasional more than friendly feeling for her, though to be perfectly honest, I never did anything about it. I say that not to impress you with what a faithful husband I was (I wasn't, and neither was my ex-wife, for that matter) but by way of letting you know that I always felt that if I did get involved with this woman, there'd be nothing casual about it. And, of course, as things turned out, I was exactly right, because when we finally did get together, it got pretty intense pretty quickly. Her name then was Diana Cooper. It's Diana Barkin now, but I'm getting ahead of myself.

Diana had this little house in Sherman Oaks, just south of Ventura Boulevard, up in the hills. It was small but really warm and cheerful, and in contrast to the dump I was living in, it was no contest. I wound up spending a lot of my nights there, and I can't remember a time in my entire life I was happier. I'm not going to embarrass Diana (who I used to call Lady Di, until that poor soul's unfortunate accident soured us both on the nickname) by telling you what a great lover she is, but I will tell you this: in my whole life, I never had sex with anyone like I had with her. First of all, she was beautiful. Tall, thin (but not skinny), with incredible legs, a gorgeous ass, and small, perfecto tits (which, like most women, she wishes were bigger but which I think are perfect just as is, having had my fill of ample breasts over the years).

She had bright blue eyes and soft blond hair, and she could take a punch. (I'm not kidding. She had a little detour on the bridge of her nose from the time her first husband took a swing at her and broke it. She dumped him the same day—she's definitely not one of those women who stick around to take a beating.)

Frankly, the fact that she was unattached amazed me: she was, as I said, very sexy, very bright, and very capable, having started her career as a lawyer in business affairs before sliding sideways into development. Plus, she made a hell of a good living.

Anyway, we'd been good friends for a couple of years, though my ex-wife, along with probably all of Diana's girlfriends, thought we were already fucking our brains out. Vicariously, their husbands probably hoped so. Anyway, I finally said to her, as long as we've been convicted of the crime, we may as well commit it, and that's what we did. And Jesus Christ—it was like a dam bursting or something. We couldn't get enough of each other, which was how I came to be spending more time at her house than my own (which never really felt like my own anyway, and which I got out of the second the lease was up).

Diana had this dog, a white Lab named Bob, who was about three years old when we started living together. Bob was a great dog. You'd throw a tennis ball, he'd be all over it. He'd bring it back to you, tail going a mile a minute, but then he wouldn't let go of it. So you'd have to throw a second ball, which he'd also stuff into his mouth— now he'd have two of 'em in there—so you could pull out the first one. He loved to play, he didn't have a mean bone in him, and other than chasing down tennis balls or any other goddamn thing you threw, he lived to eat. And I don't think it's disrespectful to say that by and large, sweet as Labs are, intellect isn't exactly their strong suit, though every time I'd suggest that Bob was a little, you know, dim, Diana'd get all over me, so I don't say it to her anymore.

One night, around two-thirty in the morning, I got up to pee, and I knew as soon as I got back into bed that I was shot for the night. There I was, lying in bed, wide awake, trying not to disturb Diana, who was fast asleep next to me. Bob was on the floor farting up a brown windstorm, and I finally figured I'd go down to the kitchen and work on a script I was writing—without much enthusiasm, I might add. Of course, when I got out of bed and went downstairs, Mr. Gasbag thought there'd be some food in it for him, so he followed me down. And because he really was a good dog and he had these big, chocolate brown eyes and this cute way of cocking his head whenever he thought he might score something to eat, I went into the cupboard and got him a pig's ear, which happened to be one of his major all-time faves.

So while he was crunching away, I sat down at the kitchen table with a legal pad and a couple of Berol 350's and started writing.

I want to digress for a minute and tell you something about writing. Every once in a while, you have an idea for something that's really exciting, that really means something to you. Maybe it's something of a thematic nature, maybe it's just a good story that you've found a quirky point of view on or a great character or whatever. But when that happens, writing is the most unbelievably satisfying thing you can do, and when you're not doing it, all you can think about is getting back to it. But then there are the times (most of the time, actually, at least for me) when writing is just a job. You're a hired gun on someone else's show, you're not emotionally invested in it, and the only thing you've really got to bring to the party is your pride in your craft and your work ethic, both of which really get challenged in the face of knowing that whatever you write is going to disappear down the rat hole of someone else's creative invention anyway. And if you can still maintain your spirit, your humor, and your goodwill toward the work in spite of that, then you can call yourself a pro.

I'd been working in television for over twenty years, and I'd always prided myself on being the consummate professional. In all those years, I'd created and produced several pilots, none of which sold, and I always tried to keep at bay the thought that I simply wasn't good enough to take that next step—to be one of the select few, like John Wells or Dick Wolf or David E. Kelley, who could walk into some network head's office, spin him a ten-minute yarn, and walk out of the room with a thirteen-episode on-air commitment.

Anyway, it's in the context of that commitment to professionalism that I found myself in Diana's kitchen at two-thirty in the morning, working on my script, when the weirdest thing that ever happened to me in my whole life occurred. I'm sitting at the table scribbling scenes longhand when Bob—this is the dog, remember—says to me, out loud, in English:

"What are you writing?"

Just like that. Startled, I looked down at Bob, and he looked back at me and said it again: "What are you writing?"

Jesus Christ. I almost jumped out of my skin. "Are you talking to me?" I say.

"Well, yeah," he says, looking at me like I usually look at him, which is to say he's looking at me like I'm the dumbest creature in the room. "Who else is here?"

At this point, let me clarify what I mean when I say Bob spoke to me. His lips didn't move, like you see in those Disney movies where they animate the animals' mouths so they're actually talking, and the joke is that their lips are moving and forming words just like ours do, and it's so cute and goofy you can't help laughing, and your kids eat it up. This was different. It was more like telepathy. No lip movement whatsoever. But I swear—Bob looked at me, and there was something in his eyes I'd never seen before: a focus, an intelligence, an awareness that, coming from a dog, was the spookiest thing I'd ever experienced in my life. Nothing—I mean nothing—was even a close second to this, including the time I ran out of the Schuyler Theater on Columbus Avenue in the middle of a matinee showing of Dr. Jekyll and Mr. Hyde when I was eight years old and slept with a light on in my room for about three years.

Again: "What are you writing?"

"A TV script," I say very quietly, hoping Diana won't wake up, come down to the kitchen, and see me talking to her dog.

"I have an idea for a movie," Bob says. "Wanna hear it?"

Now I think I'm losing my mind. I can hear Bob talking to me like a human being, totally conversational, as if he does it all the time, except his lips aren't moving and he's a goddamn dog lying on the floor looking up at me. I figure, Okay, maybe I'm in some weird late-night zone or maybe it's one of those crazy dreams where you think you're awake

*but you're actually still in the dream and you don't
know it, because it's so real. So I figure: That's what
it is, and I'll go along with it. So in that spirit, I ask
him a few questions back—like, how long has he
been able to talk?*

*"I don't know," Bob says. "Since I was about
two maybe."*

"How come you never talked before?" I ask.

*"I talk all the time," Bob says. "It's just no one
ever heard me before. This is the first time."*

*"What about Diana, did you ever try talking to
her?" I ask.*

*"All the time," Bob says, "but she doesn't hear
me." Then he tells me again that he has an idea for
a movie, and do I want to hear it?*

*Hey, it's a dream, right? So I say sure and put
down my pad and pencil: Tell me. Now Bob lifts his
head up off his paws and kind of leans against the
kitchen cabinet, getting comfortable. And this is the
story—paraphrased, obviously—he tells me . . .*

It's called First Dog. It's about the president's
dog, Bob (who else?), who, through an accidental
brush with a top-secret scientific experiment, gains
the power of intellect and speech and winds up running for president (and winning) when his master
reluctantly leaves the White House after serving
two terms.

After Bob wins the election, he slowly begins losing his powers of speech and intellect, reverting, inevitably, to his pure canine nature.

Bob tells me he hasn't figured it out scene for
scene—he doesn't think he could do that—but

here's some story stuff that'd go into it. Candidate Bob would be challenged in the courts on constitutional grounds: age, species, etc. His lawyers would argue that he's the right age (in dog years), he's an American through and through, and that nowhere in the Constitution does it specifically forbid a dog from seeking the presidency.

The case would finally go to the Supreme Court, where the deciding vote would be cast by the most conservative justice, ninety-six-year-old Antonin Scalopini, who sees in Bob the reincarnation of his own beloved dog, Bruce, who is infirm and dying. Amazingly, Bob is legally accredited by the high court, runs for president, and wins in a landslide.

President Bob finds the country is in a total mess, the government's gone to hell, and in the prevailing atmosphere of cynicism and corruption, Bob reestablishes the sense of dignity, simplicity, and purpose that has, at its best, always defined the American people.

In the course of Bob's first term in office, he gives inspiring State of the Union addresses, presides over brilliant state dinners, brokers peace agreements between nations, manages to bring out the love in all those nasty senators and congressmen, and brokers consensus in a divided nation. He also finds time to fall in love with a beautiful chocolate Lab named First Lady, and together they bring harmony to the chronic racial divide.

Then, as Bob's powers begin to fade toward the end of his first term, his aides are terrified that they'll all lose their power as well. All the worst impulses in these political creatures resurface, and in his last days informed by speech and intellect, Bob teaches them the most valuable lesson of all: that what he's brought to the country need not disappear just because he's losing his wondrous powers; that the lessons outlive the dog; that the country can go on to greater good regardless of whether Bob is president or not.

Guilty of the only lie he's ever told, Bob runs for reelection, knowing he's losing his chops (as it were) but not telling the American people.

Barely weeks into his second term, Bob passes the mantle of the presidency to the vice-president, who maybe was the White House kennel guy, and in his last coherent speech tells the nation that even though he cannot serve out his term, he won't be gone. He'll be there (literally) for the next president's fireside chats, and even as he loses human intellect, his presence (along with that of First Lady) will be a constant reminder of all they were able to accomplish.

Probably the last scene is something like the inauguration of the next president, with Bob there by his side, just being . . . lovable, slobbering Bob. FADE OUT . . .

Okay, now put yourself in my shoes for a minute. You're sitting in the kitchen, it's after three in the morning, and your girlfriend's dog has just told you an idea for an entire movie.

"So what do you think?" Bob asks me. "Does it

have legs?" And, I swear to Christ, he kind of chuffed at his own joke.

By now I'm so fucked-up I don't know what to do, so I tell him, yeah, it's a pretty good idea, it's obviously a kids' movie, Disney maybe, maybe animated, I gotta think about it, maybe we should turn in, sleep on it, blah blah blah.

"Okay," Bob says. "No problem. If you like it, it's yours." And he gets up, pads over to his water bowl, takes a few laps, and goes upstairs to bed.

I could tell he was disappointed. I wanted to follow him, tell him it was an excellent idea, it's just that I'm more of a realistic drama–type writer, plus I don't have a lot of experience listening to movie pitches from a dog. But I didn't. I thought it was a better idea to go back up to bed, sleep for a couple of hours, and, in the cold light of day, reassess what I'd just been through. Assuming, that is, I even remembered it, which, I gotta tell you, I was more than half hoping I wouldn't. And of course I swore to myself that I'd never say a word about what happened to a living soul. I mean, would you? Especially not to Diana, who I'm pretty sure would have sent me packing, or at least sent me off to the puzzle house for extended observation.

As Dennis sips from the last of his coffee, now gone cold, the narrative tightens into a truncated shorthand, sort of a writer's blueprint for the remainder of the story, which reads like this:

Ron Barkin never writes the dog story. But one sleepless night, at the kitchen table again, the dog winds up telling him another story, which Ron likes a lot better, about a college professor who everyone thinks is a drunk but who's secretly a spy, and of course he's got this dog named Bob.

Ron loses the dog, and turns that story into the hit series Sleeper *and winds up making millions of dollars, plus a huge three-series deal with NBC. He marries Diana, moves into a big new house in the Palisades, and gets another dog for Bob, who never talks to him again.*

Anyway, after one particularly long and hard production season, Ron invites his tennis pro (a wanna-be writer) to house-sit while he and Diana go to Hawaii for a much needed vacation.

Two weeks later, Ron comes home, returns to work. Life couldn't be better. He's a huge success, and it's easy to forget where all that success came from. I mean, who'd believe it anyway? Plus, Ron's come to believe that the dog didn't really talk to him at all, that in the silence of the night, he plugged into a channel in his own mind where he was able to access his own best ideas, and maybe in that different space, or zone, he imagined his own writer's voice coming out of the dog.

Except for this: about four months later, after a Sunday-morning tennis game, the pro tells Ron he's got some fantastic news. He sold a screenplay.

No shit, Ron says. Who to?

Disney, says the pro.

Hey, no shit, that's fantastic. What is it?

It's a kids' movie, basically, but I think adults will like it too.

What's it about?

It's about this talking dog who becomes president of the United States . . .

Later that night, in the kitchen, two A.M., Ron looks at the dog. They haven't spoken in almost two years.

You told the tennis pro your idea, didn't you?

Yes. I thought he'd like it.

Well, he did. He sold it to Disney. It's going to be a movie.

That's good, Bob says. I always liked that one.

How come you haven't talked to me the last two years?

I talk to you all the time, Bob says. You just haven't been listening. So Sleeper really hit it big, huh?

Yeah, the writer says. It sure did.

How come you didn't keep the dog?

I don't know—it's an action-adventure show. The dog kind of got in the way. I guess I should I have thanked you, Ron says, but over time, I wasn't sure it had really even happened.

Well it did, Bob says, and if you're interested, I've got a coupla more stories I'd be happy to tell you.

Ron says, Sure, fire away.

Well, Bob says, there's this one idea I've been working on, it's about this tough cop who gets blinded in a gun battle, and he's too young to retire, he still wants to be a cop, so he gets this guide dog named Bob . . .

*   *   *

Dennis laughs out loud. Fucking writers, he thinks, chucking the story onto his desk and going for a fresh cup of coffee. Where do they come up with this shit?

Back at his desk, Dennis dials Bobby's phone number, and when Bobby picks up, Dennis says, without preamble, "You're a fucking idiot."

"What? Who is this?"

"It's Dennis the cop, and you're a fucking idiot."

"Why?"

"I read your story."

"Oh," Bobby says, disappointed. "You hated it, huh?"

"I didn't hate it," Dennis says. "It's interesting, kind of like a fiction sandwich."

"What's that mean?" Bobby asks.

"You've got the first story, about the writer with the talking dog, who's kind of like a genie in a lamp—I'll give you three wishes—and the writer takes the dog's idea and winds up rich and successful beyond his wildest dreams, and that's the top piece of bread. Then you've got the *dog's* story, about running for president and all that shit, which is the meat in the middle, and then you've got the cute little ending, where the tennis pro steals the movie idea from the dog and sells it to Disney, which is the bottom piece of bread."

"Yeah well, that's a very good analysis of the story, Detective, but did you *like* it?"

"Yeah, but I'd lose the bread and turn the meat into a movie script. I think you could sell it."

"Then how come I'm a fucking idiot?"

"You mean specifically or generally?" Dennis says.

"Asshole."

"You're a fucking idiot *specifically* because you just threw away the best cop show idea I ever read, and you didn't even realize it."

"*What* cop show idea?" Bobby asks, starting to get exasperated.

"The one about the young cop who gets blinded."

There's a pause, and then Bobby's tone changes. "Really?"

"*That's* the idea you oughta be pitching to HBO. It's different. Here's this cop, a real tough first-guy-through-the-door type, very physical, hot-tempered, doesn't hesitate to get in your face, and suddenly he's blind, and if he still wants to be a cop, he's got to learn how to use his brains, because he can't just muscle people anymore. Plus, he's got to rely on other people in a way he never did before, and it makes him emotionally vulnerable, not to mention he's completely dependent on the dog."

"So you play his emotional adjustment, how he has to turn his handicap into an asset," Bobby says. "He's got to learn to trust—his senses, his dog, other people—"

"Exactly right, numb nuts. Now you got a game."

"Jesus Christ," Bobby says. "You're right. I am a fucking idiot. That's a *great* idea."

"If you say so yourself," Dennis says.

"When do you want to sit down and lay it out?" Bobby asks, feeling the little tingle behind his eyes that's usually a surefire signal that an idea is going to turn into some serious loot.

"Anytime. You tell me."

"I can't today," Bobby says. "I got a lunch date at the Ivy, then some other stuff I have to do this afternoon, but how about dinner tomorrow night?"

"Leave me a message where and what time," Dennis says, "and I'll be there. Should I bring a pad and pencil?"

"No, you don't need to do that," Bobby says, too excited to realize Dennis is fucking with him.

Hanging up, Dennis rummages around on his desktop for Vee's eight-by-ten and dials her cell phone number. When she picks up, he says "Hi, Vee, it's Dennis Farentino, how are you?"

"Oh, *hi,*" she says, and he can hear the pleasure in her voice because he called. "I was thinking maybe you'd lost my number, or just lost interest."

"No chance of that," he says. "What happens when I meet a woman I really like is, I usually wait a week. Then, if I'm still thinking about her, I know I'm not wasting my time."

"Thank you, Detective, I'm flattered."

"So, you want to get some dinner sometime?"

"I'd love to."

"Tonight?"

"I can't tonight," Vee says, sounding genuinely disappointed. "What about tomorrow night?"

"Lemme check my calendar a minute, hold on," Dennis says, then counts to ten in his head before saying, "Yeah, tomorrow's good. How about I pick you up around seven-thirty?"

"Great," Vee says. "I'm staying with my friend Lisa Jacoby at 8221 Norton Avenue, it's a block north of Santa Monica Boulevard."

"Great. I can't wait," says Dennis.

"Me either," says Vee. "Really."

Now Dennis has to call Bobby back and tell him something came up for tomorrow night that he's got to take care of—would it be all right if they had dinner the night after?

Bobby says he can't imagine anything more important than figuring out the story about the blind cop, that it's only going to make them a million bucks, but if that's the way Dennis wants to be, okay, they can do it the night after.

CHAPTER 20

Dennis's enthusiasm for the blind-cop idea has inspired Bobby. It *is* a better idea than the other one. It's more original, and even though there's still plenty of room for action, there's also the more thoughtful kind of detective work Dennis was talking about. The beauty of it is, it's character-driven, and the character is Dennis. Bobby *knows* he can write it, and the certain knowledge of it makes him smile. He's hot and he knows it.

Getting ready to meet Linda at the Ivy, Bobby's feeling better than he's felt in years. Sure there's still an ache when he thinks about Vee, but more important, he's writing for the first time in over a year, really writing, not just hack rewrites for the money, and it's going great. He's inside Linda's head, he and Dennis have really hit it off, the screenplay inspired by having seen Ramon's murder is maturing nicely, and he loves the fact that the story is playing itself out in real time, that instead of being some contrived piece of crap like most of what he does, this one is true.

The only downside is that if Dennis stalls on the murder investigation, Bobby may have to help things along, and if that means he's got to give Linda up, then so be it, he'll live with it. Shit, how's it different than if he'd called 911 as soon as he saw the murder?

And because Bobby's a writer and he's used to having conversations with himself, he lets himself answer the question.

Of course it's different, asshole. The difference being if you'd called right away, you'd have been reporting a crime, whereas now, you're betraying a woman you're having an affair with under false pretenses.

A distinction without a difference, Bobby tells his contrary self. The result is the same whether he did it then or does it now, and the result is all that matters. Besides, how can something that would've been right then not be right now?

In the silence that follows, with Bobby satisfied that his moral compass is still pointing true north, he finishes dressing and heads off to the Ivy.

Over lunch and a bottle of wine, Bobby and Linda find themselves intoxicated not only by the wine but by the excitement of clandestine romance (is there anything sexier?).

Barely touching his food, Bobby never takes his eyes from Linda, telling her how attracted he is to her—that it's not only the sex, which ("don't get me wrong") is great, but their synchronicity—that incredible feeling that, in all the important ways, they click. Both of them are tough, smart, quick-witted, and opportunistic—but they're also caring, sensitive, and giving, always searching for the right someone to be with, and to love.

Linda reaches over to take Bobby's hand, not caring who's watching. And, trust me, people are watching. "Listen to me," she says, with surprising urgency. "In all the years I've been married to Marv, this is the first time I've ever been truly unfaithful."

Off Bobby's understandable skepticism, she explains that she's not talking about sexual fidelity. Marv lost sexual interest in her years ago, as his tastes got, shall we say, more exotic. Linda tells Bobby that while she and Marv never talked about it, she always assumed that at some point Marv realized she was discreetly taking care of her own needs and didn't care, as long as it stayed pretty much in the same category (for Marv) as taking a crap. It was something you needed to do on a regular basis, but you didn't talk about it, you did it in private (even if you *were* using a whore as your toilet), and you cleaned up afterward.

Marv was the kind of guy who could split his sexual self off from the rest of him, and he expected Linda to do the same, an expectation she always thought was fair, given that she'd made the deal in the first place. And so her affairs were discreet (at least until the one with Ramon, Bobby's thinking), they were emotionally undemanding, and in her

way she was as true to Marv as he was to her—until
now, with Bobby Newman, who, she's beginning to
think, might turn into something more than a quick
flop in the feathers.

"I'm going to say something I might regret later,"
she tells him, "but I think I could fall in love with
you. Maybe I'm feeling that way because I'm a little loaded, but maybe also I'm a little loaded because I trust you. Either way, you make me feel like
anything is possible, and I didn't think I still had
that in me."

Most men would be thrilled to hear those words
from a woman of Linda Paulson's wealth and
beauty, drunk or sober. But for Bobby, it's an emotional complication he hadn't anticipated. It's one
thing to betray a woman you're having a meaning-
less fling with—you play, you pay—but it's something else again to cold-bloodedly give her up after
she's told you she might be falling in love with you.

It's an index of just how smart Linda is that she
tells Bobby she's not looking for an equivalent dec-
laration from him. She understands their situations
are totally different, that Bobby's still bruised from
his marital breakup. Linda guesses that (at least on
Bobby's side of the bed) it wasn't a loveless union
and that Bobby needs to heal before he can move
on. Linda's simply letting him know where her
head is—between his legs, if that's all he wants, but
willing to risk taking it farther north if, or when,
he's so inclined.

CHAPTER 21

THE DIFFERENCE BETWEEN A GREAT ATHLETE AND A merely average one is, the great athlete *sees* better than the average athlete. For the athlete so gifted, the game slows down. The ball looks bigger. And while everyone else is rushing, lunging, or overreacting, the great ones are lying back, seeing the whole field, letting the game come to them.

A great detective essentially does the same thing. And because Dennis is a great detective, he instinctively knows several things. He knows, for instance, that whoever killed Ramon isn't a flight risk. He also knows that whoever killed Ramon isn't likely to kill anyone else. And finally, he knows that Bobby Newman is the key to unraveling the mystery and that if he's patient—if he lets the game come to him, in other words—the pieces of the puzzle will come together and the big picture will reveal itself. It's sort of like painting by numbers, except you have to figure out which numbers go where before you can apply the colors.

Which is why Dennis, off Bobby's inadvertent slip regarding specific knowledge of the murder weapon, has been staked out across the street from Bobby's house for the last couple of hours, and before that at the Ivy as well, watching and waiting. And when the front door opens to reveal Linda and Bobby, he watches them embrace and kiss, without question lovers.

Linda hurries to her car and drives off, Bobby closes the door, and Dennis counts to ten slowly before driving off too, pleased the game is finally beginning to come his way.

CHAPTER 22

BOBBY SPENDS THE REMAINDER OF THE DAY WRITING, takes a dinner break, then goes back to writing until well past midnight before turning in for eight hours of uninterrupted sleep, a welcome change from the nights he'd sleep two or three hours, wake up with a pounding headache, then doze fitfully on and off until daylight.

The next morning, Bobby showers, shaves, puts on a fresh pair of jeans with a clean white shirt, and checks himself out in the full-length mirror behind the bathroom door, liking what he sees. He realizes that for a guy heading out to meet his wife and her divorce attorney for a preliminary settlement conference, he's happier than he's been in a very long time. He's working again, his relationship with Dennis—which he initiated under, let's face it, false pretenses—has become something more like a genuine friendship (which may become unexpectedly profitable for both of them), *and* he's having an affair with a gorgeous woman, who makes him feel sexy and attractive again.

This is not to suggest that Bobby doesn't miss Vee. In point of fact Bobby misses her a lot, and the reason he's not showing up at this meeting with his own attorney is not just that he doesn't want to give Vee half of everything he's earned since they got married. He also continues to hold out some hope that given his rejuvenated state, Vee will want to give the marriage another chance. But you know how just when you start thinking you're really on a roll life suddenly kicks you right in the ass, just to let your Secret Self know that you really *are* the worthless piece of shit you've always tried to talk yourself out of believing you are?

Well, that's what happens to Bobby when he goes to meet with Vee and her lawyer, Howard Bornstein, a loathsome, smug little weasel with a bad hairpiece—redundant, I realize. (What is it with these guys anyway? Do they think people can't tell that the thing slapped on top of their head isn't real? Do they think it somehow makes them more attractive to women? More successful in business? Jesus Christ, they'd be ugly if they had *real* hair. Then again, who knows? Maybe they look in the mirror and say to themselves, "Goddamn, you look great.")

In any event, the first thing out of Vee is "Where's your lawyer?"

"How about, 'Hello, Bobby, nice to see you,

Bobby, how are you, Bobby,' *then* 'Where's your lawyer?' " Bobby says, trying not to sound too pissed off too soon.

Fat chance of that.

Now Howard the weasel says, "Mr. Newman, it's my experience that usually, when one of the parties to a divorce shows up without their attorney, there's a reluctance to deal forthrightly with the reality of the situation."

To which Bobby says, "The reality of the situation, at least for me, is that I'd like a chance to get my wife back."

"Howard, I'm not going to sit here and put up with this," says Vee. "Would you please tell him that he's not going to get his wife back, his wife has left the building and wants a divorce, and nothing he says or does is going to change that?"

"Goddamnit, Vee, don't talk to him like I'm not in the fucking room! We were married for six years. We *loved* each other. I *still* love you. Look at me!"

"Mr. Newman," the weasel says, trying to regain control of the room. "Your wife has made it very clear she has no interest in a reconciliation. So if you really do love her, you'll leave now, retain counsel for yourself, and reschedule this meeting at a later date."

"Mr. Bornstein," Bobby says very politely, "shut up and kiss my ass." Then, to Vee: "I'm writing again. I've cleaned up my act drinking-wise. I sold a pitch to New Line. I'm working on an original screenplay that's really good. I have an HBO project in the works. I admit I was a pain in the balls there for a while, but that's over with, I swear. All I'm asking for is a chance. I'll even go to therapy."

"No," says Vee. "How many languages do I have to say 'it's over' in?"

"How many languages do I have to say 'I love you' in?" Bobby asks. "Even if you have fucked around on me and treated me like a piece of shit, which maybe I deserved, the point is, things have changed. *I've* changed."

"That's good. I'm glad for you. But I've changed, too. I don't love you anymore. I just want to get a divorce now and move on with my life."

"Just like that."

Now Vee starts to get emotional. "Not *just like that*. After six years. After trying, after *begging* you to get therapy. After the drinking, after the mood swings, after the belittling, after waiting patiently, hoping you'd snap out of it, hoping you'd start treating me like a woman again instead of a *thing* walking around in your house—you'd have treated a stranger better than you treated me! I want my life back, Bobby. I want to be with someone who cares about me, supports me, encourages me! Someone who wants to share a life with me!"

"Does Jared fucking Axelrod want to share a life with you? Is he dumping his wife for you? Now that you're out there on your own, not having to sneak around behind your husband's back, is he still returning your calls? Is he still throwing a hump into you every day at the Peninsula Hotel?"

"You're *such* a loser," Vee spits at him. "You'll always be a loser!"

"Hey, I'm not the one living in some shitty Hollywood apartment waiting for my married boyfriend to call."

"Go fuck yourself," Vee shouts, and storms out of the conference room, leaving Bobby for the second (and, you better believe it, last) time.

The door slams like a rifle shot, but Bornstein is unfazed. "Get an attorney, Mr. Newman. Have him call me." And he gathers up his papers and exits, leaving Bobby alone in the conference room.

Bobby chases him out into the reception area. "I wouldn't be surprised if you're throwing a hump into her too, you rat-headed little prick!" he shouts at the guy's back, and the receptionist at the front desk has to duck her head under the desk so that no one will see her laughing her ass off.

So much for the settlement conference.

Back home, and for the first time since the night of Ramon's murder, Bobby slips the tape of Vee and Ramon into the VCR and watches it obsessively, over and over. Jealous rage consumes him like a grease fire, helping to cook an idea that has taken hold in his mind like a fast-spreading cancer, until the idea finally hatches, giving birth to a full-fledged plan.

What Bobby does next you can probably chalk up to a desire for revenge against a woman he believes has humiliated and belittled him. You can also chalk it up to having about five scotches and getting shit-faced, because if he's anywhere *near* sober, he never pulls this kind of stunt to begin with. But hey.

CHAPTER 23

I'M PROBABLY ON SHAKY GROUND TRYING TO IDENTIFY the human condition based on my own less than extensive observations over the course of my time on the planet. That said, my guess is that secrets and their attendant shame tend to determine the basic formation of our character and are, by and large, why shrinks make such a good living. Some people feel powerful holding on to secrets, but I think most of us are ashamed of them.

In the privacy of your own mind, think about your trunk full of secrets, dating back as far as earliest childhood, when you wet the bed. Or later, when you stole money from your folks. Or locked yourself in the can to spank your monkey. Or took the family car without permission.

How about the first time you had sex? If you're

looking for a petri dish of secrets in which to breed
a little shame and guilt, look no further.

By the time we reach adulthood, we're freighted
with so many secrets we can barely keep track of
them, or the lies that surround them like so many
sentries. You're gay. You're impotent. You have
herpes. You're screwing your trainer. Or your husband's boss. Or your wife's best friend. You're a
drunk. A degenerate gambler. You've stolen from
the company you work for.

A lot of people think it takes courage to confess
one's secrets. Personally, I've always felt it takes
more courage *not* to confess. People usually confess
stuff because their secrets weigh too heavily, and
rather than do the hard work of changing, so
they'll never behave that way again, they spill their
guts, hoping to be forgiven so they can fill up their
tank with more guilty secrets.

Where's the courage, for instance, in telling your
wife you got your cock sucked by two whores at a
business convention? Or telling her you're fucking
your secretary? (It's not like telling your priest,
who, from what I read of late, has his own issues
with secrecy.)

Your wife, if you're lucky, may not beat your
brains out forever, but I promise she'll never let you
up (or trust you ever again) completely. Which
doesn't mean she may not have secrets of her own
(she probably does). It just means she has the
courage to keep them to herself.

My first marriage was like a training bra. Not
very sexy, but it held us up until we grew out of it.

Along the way, my ex-wife screwed around a little, I screwed around a little, and we both made the mistake of confessing our affairs to each other, as if that would wipe the slate clean. A couple of miserable years later, we threw in the towel.

My current wife, of sixteen years (two great kids, so far so good, knock on wood and spit three times), and I have no particular secrets (at least none that I know of), but you know what? I don't want to hear what she did or whom she did it with before we were married, and vice versa. Who needs the snapshots?

I think I said earlier that my wife and I always tried to teach our kids not to lie, the reward for which being, among other things, that you never have to remember what you said. But it's naïve to think that by the time you teach it to them they don't already have more secrets than they know what to do with, or that they don't think you're a hypocrite for lecturing them on something you're not capable of yourself.

In my experience, what takes the most courage of all is to genuinely forgive, particularly someone you love, and find it in your heart to reinvest the trust that's been embezzled from your account.

I say all this because every rare once in a while, these are issues that resonate on a first date. Most first dates are sparring sessions. A man and a woman feel each other out, tell each other their well-practiced lies, and generally decide whether it's worth it to go somewhere and fuck. People do it all the time. They do it because they're lonely, bored, full of self-loathing, or sometimes just too insecure to say no. But rarely do they do it because they're mutually, genuinely attracted to each other. On those rare occasions, when there's real potential for alchemy, the magic of chemistry and compatibility between a man and a woman, things usually slow down. The couple knows instinctively that there's more at stake, hence more to lose, by going too quickly.

With all this in mind, consciously or unconsciously, Dennis and Vee are on their first date, having dinner at a restaurant called Chianti, on Melrose Avenue in Hollywood. And almost from the start there's a little magic between them (chalk it up to those pesky pheromones), and a feeling on both their parts that they want to treat each other with a little extra care. Which means that while Vee sanitizes her life story for Dennis's benefit, she doesn't try to pretend she's a virgin. At thirty-two, even accounting for her six years with Bobby, she's had a life she's more or less unashamed of.

But she does have her secrets. She can live with her stupid one-nighter with Ramon, partly because it was just about sex, but mostly because he's dead and it won't come back to bite her. Her affair with Axelrod is another matter. It's not about love or the sex, which pretty much is what it is, but more about his power and her need to access it; also, he's married (as was she), which makes it a guilty pleasure and a shameful secret. And she'll admit, if only to herself, that the reason she went off on Bobby this afternoon in her lawyer's office is that he was right. Axelrod *is* a prick. He was using her, and now that she's left her husband, suddenly her phone calls aren't being returned and those afternoons at the Peninsula are a thing of the past.

What she does tell Dennis about is her childhood growing up in Pittsburgh, her two years at Carnegie-Mellon in the theater department, her career ups and downs, and her marriage ups and downs with Bobby, which, for the last couple of years, were mainly downs. She says she hasn't lost a moment's sleep over her decision to leave the marriage, and as much as she'll always care for Bobby, that part of her life is behind her. This by way of letting Dennis know that she's not some miserable, rebounding broad looking to get distracted by a fling with a good-looking homicide detective.

As for Dennis, he's a professional custodian of secrets, his own and others'. (You wouldn't believe the things people have confessed to him: rapes, murders, torture killings, beheadings. One man calmly told Dennis how he'd cut off the hands, the feet, and the head of his homosexual lover, then sat the naked torso in a chair with its head facedown in its lap, its hands and feet neatly displayed on the floor below. Then, so relieved to have unburdened himself of his secret, he fell asleep right there at the interrogation table.)

That said, he's probably more candid with Vee than he's been with any woman he can remember. Of course, he doesn't tell her about his relationship with Bobby. Nor does he tell her about Bobby's affair with Linda Paulson. And you better believe he doesn't say anything regarding the fact that her (soon to be ex-) husband is the key to puzzling out Ramon's murder, he's just not sure how yet.

What he *does* tell her (honestly) is that from the moment he saw her picture, he wanted to meet her, and from the moment he met her he wanted to be with her, not as a euphemism for sex, but literally, as in *be* with her: sit with her, talk to her, get to know her, share stuff with her, watch her laugh, enjoy looking at her. He tells her about his two failed marriages, admitting that their failure was pretty much his fault. He was just no good at it, he says, any more than he was at a subsequent series of casual romances that went nowhere because, among other reasons, the women always seemed to think Dennis needed a little changing here and there. "In fact," he tells Vee, "listening to myself talk, you might want to change your phone number after tonight."

Vee laughs, then tells Dennis not to worry. "I like you just the way you are. I was disappointed when you didn't call and excited when you did. I like your eyes, I like that you're a cop—don't ask me why, I don't know yet—and I'm not going to try to change anything about you. I'm also not going to sleep with you tonight, because I like you enough that I want to go slow."

"Sort of let the game come to us," Dennis says, hoping Vee knows what the hell he's talking about.

"Exactly," she says, giving him that smile that puts a little ache in him he never thought he'd feel again.

The rest of dinner is a happy mix of good wine,

good food, and the discovery that you're with someone you feel you've known forever, even though this is your first time together.

In the car, on the way back to Vee's apartment, Dennis pulls over to the curb suddenly and puts the car in park. "Listen, can I say something to you?"

Vee turns and looks at him.

"I want to see you again. Tomorrow, if I can. And the day after that. And I'm okay with the no-sex-right-away thing. We'll get to that when we get to it. But I want to kiss you, if it's all right, and I figured I'd do it now so we wouldn't have to dance around it when we get back to your place."

Vee slides into his arms, and they kiss. We've all experienced that kiss, so I don't need to describe it, except to say it seems to last forever, it's over too soon, and you know the moment your lips meet that you've set sail on a great adventure, with a warm, sweet-scented, intoxicating wind at your back.

CHAPTER 24

SOME FUCKING ADVENTURE IT TURNS OUT TO BE.
The thing is, by definition you never know where adventure will take you, and I can guarantee you that not even Dennis could've predicted what Bobby would be doing while Dennis is romancing his (soon to be ex-) wife.

Properly loaded, having had his fill of scotch and videotapes, Bobby weaves his way up to the bedroom, where he rummages around in his jewelry drawer looking for the spare key to the Toyota, which Vee took when she left. Finding it, he then opens his little strongbox, the one hidden inside a phony book that sits on the shelf beside his bed, takes out five one-hundred-dollar bills and two fifties, and stuffs them into his pocket along with the car keys.

From the back of his desk drawer, Bobby retrieves Ramon's little black book, along with the videotape of Vee brushing her teeth with Ramon's dick (which he'd thought for a while he might anonymously send to Jared Axelrod).

Going to the garage, where he keeps a five-gallon can of gasoline for emergencies, Bobby puts it in the trunk of his car. Then, throwing the videotape and the little black book into the glove compartment of his Boxster, Bobby pulls the car out of the garage and heads down into Hollywood.

Hollywood Boulevard is to hookers what Van Nuys Boulevard is to used cars. Block after block of product is lined up, priced to sell according to age and condition, and in both cases, what you see isn't always what you get, the operative word being *used*. Let's just say the cautionary "buyer beware" applies big-time.

Bobby shops Hollywood Boulevard slowly until he catches the eye of a gaudily made up whore, who minces over to his car on her three-inch heels when he pulls to the curb.

Bobby opens the window on the passenger side and leans across to speak to the hooker, who bends down to check him out.

"Hey, honey," she says. "Wanna party?"

"How much for a blow job?" Bobby asks, cutting to the chase.

"How do I know you ain't a cop?"

"I'm not," Bobby tells her. "What do I have to do to prove it?"

The hooker climbs into Bobby's car and puts her hand on his crotch. "Take your thing out."

Bobby unzips his fly and pulls his dick out. "How much?"

"For that little thing?" she says, laughing, knowing no cop would expose himself like that.

"I promise you," Bobby says. "The closer it gets to your mouth, the bigger it'll look."

"Fifty."

"Okay," Bobby says, not haggling, knowing he probably could get it for twenty but happy to pay the extra thirty for the goodwill he's going to need after she blows him.

"Up front," the whore says, surprised Bobby's not looking to negotiate.

Bobby gives her the fifty, and she stuffs it into her little purse. "Drive around the corner and park up the street a ways."

Once parked, Bobby comes around to the passenger side of the car and slides in, and the whore kneels down between his legs and takes care of business.

"Now that you know I'm not a cop," Bobby says, zipping up, "how about you help me get right?"

"What've you got in mind, honey?"

"I need you to score a couple of grams of blow," Bobby says. "One for me, one for you."

"You're talkin' four, five hundred bucks," she says.

Bobby hands her the five one-hundred-dollar bills, which she quickly stuffs into her purse before he can change his mind.

"Sounds like a plan, baby," she says, not having a clue about how much of a plan it really is.

Twenty minutes later, armed with a five-gallon

can of gas, the videotape of Vee fucking Ramon, the little black book, and a gram of newly acquired coke, Bobby drives over to West Hollywood—8221 Norton Avenue, to be exact—and parks across the street from Vee's apartment complex. There's a car-port that runs the length of the building, and before Bobby gets the gasoline out of his car, he saunters over to make sure Vee's car is there, which it is.

Working quickly, Bobby unlocks her car with the spare key and sticks Ramon's little black book in the glove box, along with the videotape. Then he takes the gram of coke and drops it on the driver's seat, in plain view.

Safely back in his own car, Bobby calls 911 to report a car fire. Then, not wanting to destroy the evidence he's planted, Bobby waits until he hears the wail of sirens in the distance before quickly dousing Vee's car with gasoline and setting it on fire.

Next thing you know, two big-ass fire engines arrive on the scene, sirens wailing, and Bobby watches from a safe distance down the street as the firefighters put out the blaze before too much damage is done.

When they open the car door to drain out the water, they find the cocaine on the seat and immediately radio for the cops. It must be a slow night in West Hollywood, because within another few minutes, two sheriff's units arrive to scour the car, and it's somewhere in the midst of all this activity that Dennis and Vee arrive on the scene.

From across the street and a couple of hundred feet away, Bobby watches, first delighted, then stunned, as he sees Vee and Dennis get out of Dennis's car.

That motherfucker, Bobby thinks. *He's fucking my wife behind my back.* And whatever reservations Bobby might have had about putting Vee in a jackpot evaporate in the reflected heat of the smoldering Toyota.

Fuck both of you, Bobby thinks, and drives off, unnoticed in the commotion of deputies and firefighters surrounding Vee's car.

By now Dennis has tinned the deputies, and they show him the cocaine, telling him, almost apologetically, that they're going to have to arrest Vee and impound her car.

If you think Dennis is stunned, you should see Vee. Her car is a smoldering mess, the deputies are reading her rights to her as they put her in cuffs, and she has no idea how in hell a gram of cocaine wound up inside her car.

"Dennis, I swear, this is crazy," she pleads, terrified and in tears. "I don't use drugs. I've *never* used drugs. This has got to be a mistake!"

Her shock and distress are so genuine that even allowing for her being an actress, Dennis is inclined to believe her, and as they're putting Vee into the back of the car to take her to the West Hollywood sheriff's substation, Dennis tells her not to say a word to anyone.

But before the car pulls away, another deputy comes over to show Dennis the little black book and the videotape they found in the glove compartment. Telling the deputies that the tape and the book are important pieces of evidence in his murder investigation, he says he's going to want to question Vee down at Hollywood Division before they process her on the drug charge. And since murder trumps simple possession, Vee gets handed off to Dennis. He thanks the deputies for their cooperation and promises that as soon as he's done with her, she's all theirs.

With an odd mixture of pleasure and regret, Dennis realizes his case is back in play and that the game has finally come to him.

CHAPTER 25

It's well past midnight when Dennis shows up to relieve the night-duty detective who's been keeping an eye on Vee. Her eyes, already red and swollen from crying, well up with tears all over again.

"You've got some problems," he tells Vee.

"I know this sounds crazy," she says, "but I think Bobby put those drugs in my car."

"Why would he do that?" Dennis asks.

"Because we had a terrible fight today."

"What about?"

"He showed up at my lawyer's. It was supposed to be a settlement conference, but all he wanted to talk about was getting back together again, which I told him wasn't going to happen. He got angry, then I got angry, we called each other names, and I walked out. This is him trying to hurt me—I know it."

"Forget about the drugs," Dennis says. "That's not your problem." And the flat sound of his voice, his *cop* voice, the one she's never heard before, suddenly chills her.

"What do you mean?"

"There was also a little book in your glove compartment that belonged to Ramon Montevideo, and it lists all the women he's had sex with the last coupla years, plus his little comments about what they do and how well they do it. You're in it: oral, B-plus, screamer."

Vee's hand reflexively covers her mouth, and her eyes go wide. That's the thing about secrets. The very one she never thought would wind up biting her in the ass just has, and now the only question is, How poisonous is the venom?

"Plus," Dennis says, "there was this videotape," and he slides it out of its shiny black cardboard container.

"Oh God, no," Vee says, realizing suddenly that when Dennis had asked her if she'd ever heard that Ramon secretly taped his sexual escapades, it wasn't an idle question.

Dennis turns on the TV set and puts the tape in the VCR.

"Please don't," Vee begs him. "Please."

Dennis hits PLAY anyway, and there it is, Vee going down on Ramon, and it's the most humiliating thing she's ever seen in her life. Flooded with shame, blinded by her own tears, Vee drops her head, unable to look.

Mercifully, Dennis stops the tape, takes it out of

the machine, and puts it back in its cardboard sleeve. Handing her a box of tissues, he says, "This is where we are. You had an affair with this guy—"

"It *wasn't* an affair. It only happened once."

"Whatever. You had sex with him. He taped it. Then he winds up dead on his bedroom floor, and you have the tape, plus his little black book, in the glove compartment of your car."

"Dennis, I swear, you've got to believe me. I only had sex with him the one time. I don't know why. I guess I was angry at Bobby. Ramon made me feel attractive . . . It was stupid, I never should have done it, I was ashamed of myself then and you'll never know how ashamed and embarrassed I am now. But I didn't kill him. I had no idea that tape existed, and I never knew anything about a little black book. You've got to believe me. Please. I swear to you." And now she's looking straight at Dennis, her eyes wet with tears but steady. "I know I'm in trouble. I know you probably won't ever want to see me again. But please believe me. I don't use drugs. I didn't kill Ramon. And I have no idea how that stuff got into my car."

"Listen to me, Vee," Dennis says. "You *are* in a world of trouble. And it doesn't matter whether I believe you or not. There's enough evidence right here to indict you for murder, plus you don't have an alibi."

"Yes I do," Vee says, past being humiliated, past holding on to any reasonable expectation that Dennis will ever think she's anything more than a cheap Hollywood broad trying to fuck her way into a career she couldn't earn on the merits. And so she tells him about her affair with Jared Axelrod, about the afternoons at the Peninsula, how even Bobby will confirm it, having accidentally seen the two of them there together, which precipitated the fight that caused her to walk out on the marriage. She says she was with Axelrod in his suite at the Peninsula Hotel the night Ramon was murdered, and the reason she didn't tell Dennis is obvious. When you think you may be falling in love with one guy, you don't tell him about the affair you were having with another guy. Besides, he is married, he's got children, and she wanted to protect him and his family from an embarrassing situation.

"Are you still seeing him?" Dennis asks.

"No," Vee says. "It's over."

"I believe you," Dennis says. "But until I check it out, I can't let you go."

"Do I have to go to jail?" Vee asks.

"No. I can't let you go home, but I can keep you here for now. And if your story checks out, I'll talk to the D.A., see what we can do about the cocaine charge."

"Thank you, Dennis. And for what it's worth, I am so sorry."

"Listen to me, Vee. I'm a cop. I've seen and heard lots worse. We all do things we're ashamed of. I'm no angel myself. Okay?"

Off her grateful smile, he tells her to sit tight. And

for the first time in hours, Vee's fear and shame recede a little behind the realization that Dennis may be one of those rare men actually capable not only of understanding but of forgiving.

CHAPTER 26

AT EIGHT FORTY-FIVE IN THE MORNING, DENNIS TINS
his way onto the Fox lot and walks into Jared
Axelrod's outer office, where some hatchet-faced
secretary named Sylvia is guarding the palace gates.

"May I help you," she says, the subtext being *I
don't know who you are, you don't look like anyone important, and you are going to get in to see
my boss over my cold, dead body.*

"I'd like to talk to Mr. Axelrod for a few minutes
if you don't mind," Dennis says, showing her his
badge. "My name is Dennis Farentino."

"Mr. Axelrod's in a production meeting and can't
be disturbed. Can you tell me what it's about, and
I'll have him call you?"

Dennis smiles and says to her nicely, "Tell Mr.
Axelrod it's about a murder I'm investigating, and
if he doesn't see me right now, I'll break his door

down and drag him out to my car in handcuffs."

Now he's got her attention. She picks up her phone, punches the intercom, and says, "There's a Detective Farentino here to see you. I told him you were in a meeting, but he insists." Hanging up, she says, "Mr. Axelrod will see you." And if looks could kill, Dennis would be taking the Big Dirt Nap as we speak.

"Thanks," he says, flashing his best smile, and opens the door to Axelrod's office.

"Come on in, Detective. Jared Axelrod," he says, extending a hand. "Nice to meet you. Buy you a cup of coffee?" This said as they shake hands.

"Sure, that'd be great," Dennis says to this phony prick, hating him already. "Black."

"Sylvia! Bring the detective a cup of coffee, black!" And he gestures to the couch. "Sit down, sit down."

Dennis sits. "She said you weren't available, you were in a production meeting."

"The only meeting I was in was the meeting between my ass and my toilet seat. I was having my morning dump." And when Sylvia enters with the coffee, Axelrod says, for her benefit, "Sylvia's the Mother Superior around here. Half the time she tells *me* I'm not available."

You could crack glass with what passes for a smile on Sylvia's sour puss, but Dennis just says "Thanks" when she puts the coffee down, and both men wait until she's left and closed the door behind her before Axelrod says, "So. What can I do for you, Detective?"

And because Vee is sitting down at Hollywood

Division with her whole life up for grabs, Dennis doesn't fuck around with his Columbo act. "We need to talk about Vee Wallace," Dennis says, seeing Axelrod's eyes go momentarily wide.

"What about her?"

"You've been having an affair."

"Whoa, hold on, Detective. That is *totally* not true. I'm a married man, for God's sake. Plus, even if I weren't, she's an actress, which is kind of like shitting where you eat, if you know what I mean. Not to mention her husband's a friend of mine as well as a professional colleague."

"Don't bullshit me, Jared," Dennis says, "or the next time we talk it'll be at your house, at dinnertime, with your wife and your kids wondering what the hell some Hollywood homicide detective wants with Daddy."

"Aw, man," Jared says miserably.

"You've been observed at the Peninsula Hotel. I know you keep a suite there. I'm not looking to embarrass you, but I will unless you start telling me the truth right now."

"All right," Jared says, getting smaller in his fat, cushy chair. "We spent some time together. What's this about?"

"I'm trying to place her whereabouts on the night Ramon Montevideo was murdered."

"Jesus Christ," Axelrod says. "You're looking at *Vee*?" And Dennis is reminded of that asshole junior agent Ari Goldstein, who had pretty much the same reaction, with almost the same kind of involuntary glee.

"Were you with her that night?"

"Is she saying I was?"

"Now you're fucking with me, Jared, and I thought we were past that."

"Look, Detective, I need to know. Is this going to bite me in the ass? Because if it is—"

"How many different ways do you want me to say I'm not looking to hurt you? Besides," Dennis says, "I'm a big fan of your work."

"Okay," Axelrod says, looking marginally relieved. "We had a little thing going. You know how it is. It's not like I go looking for it, but when it drops into your lap, as it were, it's un-American to say no." Like now they're just two guys in the locker room talking about pussy.

"So you *were* with her the night Ramon was murdered."

Axelrod nods. "But it's over now, I swear," he says, adding, "I could really use a break here, Detective."

Dennis takes one last sip of coffee and stands. "Your secret's safe with me, Jared, and I appreciate your candor."

If irony were rain, Axelrod would be a drowning rat.

At the door, within earshot of Hatchet Face, Dennis says, Columbo-like, "Oh, by the way. You might want to let Sylvia know that next time I call or drop by, you'll find time for me."

CHAPTER 27

HAVE YOU EVER BOUGHT A LOTTERY TICKET? I MEAN, even if you're not a regular player, every once in a while, when the payout gets up in the mega-millions—you know, like 75, 85 million dollars—you say to yourself, What the hell, and when you're paying for breakfast up at Mort's Deli in the Palisades, you take back your change in lottery tickets.

They say your odds of winning the lottery are something on the order of 40 million to one. You have a better chance of getting hit by lightning or waking up one morning to discover that you've morphed into a fucking cockroach overnight. But you buy the tickets anyway, right? And in spite of yourself, you entertain the fantasy of what you'll do with the money when you win it.

Let's see . . . 85 million, you're going to want to take the lump-sum payout, which turns out to be

54 million or so at present-day value, then divide by two for taxes, and you're looking at 27 million bucks—net, net.

Now you start spending it. This is L.A., so you figure you could easily go 6 or 7 million for a proper home befitting your new status as a multi-millionaire, plus you've got to go another million for furnishings. Then let's say you just flat-out blow a couple of million on toys, like a Ferrari Pininfarina coupe, a world-class wine cellar, and a state-of-the-art media room. Next, subtract 10 from the 27 you started with, and you've got 17 million left. You figure, I'm not going to be an asshole. I've won the lottery. I'm set for life if I don't fuck it up. So you take the remaining 17 million and invest it in tax-frees, figuring you can live off the income for the rest of your life, except it turns out that tax-frees are as lousy an investment as everything else out there. You know what your annual yield off 17 million in tax-frees is, these days? About *175,000,* give or take.

Okay—rewind the tape. You bought a couple of lottery tickets. Inconceivably, beyond all odds, your ship came in, you won *85 million bucks,* and for all your trouble, not even counting the friends and relatives lining up with their hands out, calling you a cheap fuck for not giving them a taste, what did you wind up with? A nice house and $175,000 a year, which barely covers your property tax and maintenance. Christ, you thought you'd struck it rich, and you find out you still have to work for a living.

I guess 85 million just doesn't go as far as it used to. But you buy the tickets anyway, because you're not thinking about the practical realities of a windfall—you're just caught up in the fantasy of it. And that is why, ladies and gentlemen, notwithstanding the billion-to-one long shot, people get caught up in the dream of hitting it big in Hollywood. Fame, money, freedom, sex, power, you name it—in short, escape from the ordinary restraints of normal life—and all it takes is unusual luck, unusual beauty (big tits wouldn't hurt, either), and a willingness (eagerness, even) to fuck your buddy before he fucks you. You know the old saying—success is never so sweet as when accompanied by the failure of a friend.

So if you think of Hollywood as a never-ending lottery, in which your odds of getting hit by lightning are better than your chances of catching it in a bottle, you begin to get some sense of the jealousy, the desperation, the naked aggression you can encounter as you crawl on your belly through the vast minefield that separates you from the success you spend every waking moment of your life lusting after.

In that scenario, talent is usually secondary to ambition, and morality, to say the least, is MIA. And yet they keep on coming. I guess it's a testament to the human spirit, or maybe just the Darwinian notion of survival of the fittest. Or maybe they're both the same: excuse me, coming through, get the fuck out of my way, give me what I want or I'll take it from you.

The vast majority of people who flock to Hollywood looking to win the lottery never even get into the game. But anybody who's ever plugged away on the periphery of fame and fortune knows that if you do get a shot at it—a real, honest to God, once-in-a-lifetime shot at the brass ring—and you don't grab for it no matter what—or who—is in your way, you're a genuine, twenty-four-carat *schmuck*.

Then there's the fact that as hard as it may be to achieve success, it's even harder to maintain it. And by the same reasoning, *having* a moral compass isn't nearly as hard as holding on to it against the riptide of avarice, corruption, jealousy, envy, and general moral bankruptcy that are the hallmarks of the Hollywood entertainment industry.

Dennis will be the first one to tell you he's not exactly a choirboy. He's done things he's not proud of, personally and professionally. He's cut corners, he's violated people's rights, but he's always had a conscience, he's always known right from wrong, and when he's done wrong things, he always felt he was doing them for right reasons. Of course, rationalizing the things you do to people on the grounds that the ends justify the means is a slippery slope, and Dennis knows it.

That said, Dennis is reminded of the time he went to New York City to pick up six hundred thousand dollars *cash* for an actor friend of his, who'd won it off the bookies during an out-of-his-mind lucky weekend betting college and pro football games. The friend was scared to go himself, partly because he was a fairly well known celebrity and mostly because he was afraid someone would kill him for the money. Six hundred thousand bucks cash, in a duffel bag, is a lot of incentive. People get killed for a lot fewer zeroes than that.

So, as a favor, and against his better judgment, Dennis goes to New York, meets some wiseguy named Bogo in the hallway of an Upper West Side tenement, and takes delivery of the bag of cash, letting Bogo see the nine-millimeter Glock clipped to his belt during the exchange. Dennis checks to make sure the whole six hundred thou is in the bag, and then, as he's leaving to go back to the airport, Bogo gives him a big grin and says, "America, huh? What a country."

Indeed. And on the plane ride back to L.A., Dennis can't help contemplating all the ways he could steal the money and get away with it. It's gambling money, in cash, in a duffel bag, sitting between his feet. All he has to do is tell his friend that the bookie stiffed him. Or that three guys took him off in the hallway. Or that the money was stolen out of his hotel room. Or maybe all he has to do is look his friend in the eye and say, "What money?" What's the friend going to do about it? Not a fucking thing. Gambling is illegal, and Dennis is a cop.

Of course at the end of the day, Dennis gave his grateful friend the bag full of money, and the guy lost it all and then some the next weekend in Las Vegas, betting craps and playing blackjack.

Dennis swore to himself that if he ever got another chance at the brass ring, he wouldn't fuck it up again.

These reflections on the moral implications of

success and failure are brought to you by Dennis Farentino, ladies and gentlemen, as he winds his way up the Hollywood Hills toward Bobby's house, speed-dialing A.D.A. Lynette Alvarez as he drives.

When she comes on the line, Dennis says, "Lynnie, this is Dennis . . . I'm good. You? . . . I know, I've been jammed with this Ramon Montevideo deal . . . I know, I will, I promise. Soon. But lookit, I need you to do something for me."

And he tells her about Vee's arrest last night, how he pulled rank on the sheriff's deputies who made the bust because he needed to question her about the evidence they found in her car, separate from the drugs, which pertains to his murder investigation. "Turns out the blow was planted," Dennis says, "which I'm on my way to confirm, but in the meantime, this poor girl's still being held down at Hollywood Division, scared to death, and I'd like to get her kicked. Could you take care of that for me?"

Dennis grins. "No, I'm not banging her. I'd tell you if I was, I swear to God. Will you do this for me? Just take care of the paperwork and tell Lonnie to give her a ride home, okay? You're the best."

By now he's pulled to the curb across the street from Bobby's house.

When Bobby answers the door, Dennis looks at his day-old beard and his red, puffy eyes. "You look like shit," he says. "You also smell like shit."

"I love you too," Bobby says, and walks back into the house. Dennis follows him into the kitchen and pours himself a cup of coffee.

"Help yourself," Bobby says.

"We're in a good mood this morning."

"Fuck you very much. What do you want?"

Because he's been up all night, and because Vee's tits are still in a wringer, Dennis doesn't come sidearm.

"Where were you last night?" he asks, cutting to the chase.

"I was home, writing and drinking, then just drinking, and I passed out and here I am. Where were *you*?" Bobby asks pointedly.

Dennis can see that Bobby's going to be an ass-hole, and he's not in the mood for it.

"I got a theory. You want to hear it?"

"I love a good theory," Bobby says.

"My theory is, the night Vee left you, you were out on your deck, half shit-faced, spying on your neighbors through your telescope, and as luck would have it, you saw Ramon Montevideo get murdered, which by the way is how you knew the murder weapon was his own Alma, which was not public knowledge. And instead of reporting it, you decided to write it. But a good writer's gotta know his characters, what motivates them and so forth. So you went down to Ramon's house, you let your-self in through the bedroom door off the pool, and you found Ramon's secret video stash, plus the tape in the VCR of Ramon banging whoever it was who also killed him, which I'm guessing was your cur-rent squeeze, Linda Paulson."

Now that he's got Bobby's attention big-time, Dennis warms to his narrative. "So then you sniff around the room, find Ramon's little fuck book with your wife's name in it, rummage around till you find *her* tape, the one where she's blowing Ramon, and you split—with the little black book, the tape of your wife, and, most important of all, the tape of Linda Paulson killing Ramon. You knew you should've called the cops, but it's more fun to write it than report it. So you started a relationship with Linda. You already knew she liked to fuck around on Marv—hell, everyone in town knew that—you started a relationship with me to get the cop's point of view, and then, just when it seems like you've won the lottery, you and your wife get into a big fucking beef in her lawyer's office because you want her to come back and she doesn't want to, and because you're a sick, jealous fuck, you decide to teach her a little lesson by framing her for Ramon's murder. So you put cocaine in her car, set it on fire, and when the firemen find the coke in her car, they call the cops, and the cops find the tape and the little black book, and bingo, the cocaine's just the come-on. The jackpot is, she's arrested for murder . . . Pretty good, huh?"

Bobby shakes his head. "Amazing," he says. "You are fucking amazing." And then, "You want to hear *my* theory?"

Dennis shrugs. "Sure."

"Okay. Here's *my* theory. You interview my wife during the course of your investigation. She bats her baby blues at you like she does to every guy she ever meets and, what the hell, you're a stick man, you figure you'll take a shot. Take her out to dinner, do your bullshit Columbo thing for her, tell her about all your cases, get her home, and throw a hump into her. 'Course, when you get there, the cops and the fire trucks are all over the place, they want to arrest her 'cause of the coke they find on the seat of her car, and in the process, they also find Ramon's little book, plus the tape of Vee fucking his brains out. Ramon gave her a B-plus in oral, and you're pissed off you couldn't get a little of that yourself, maybe compare your test score against his. So you take her in, she denies everything, tells you it had to be her husband who planted the blow in her car, plus she's banging this Jared Axelrod prick, check it out, I was with him the night of the murder, she says, I swear, oh please, oh please, boo hoo, boo hoo . . . How'm I doing so far?"

"So far, you're talking yourself into getting arrested."

"For what?"

"How about for accessory to murder. Obstruction of justice. Interfering with a police investigation. Conspiracy."

"This isn't *Columbo*, Dennis. You gotta prove it, and I don't think you can."

"How about I get a warrant to seize your computer? Are you telling me that screenplay you're writing isn't going to give me the proof I'm looking for?"

Shit. The screenplay.

"So here's the deal," Dennis says. "First of all, I want twenty-five percent of whatever you sell your screenplay for, plus I want shared story credit. Second of all, you tell me everything, right this fucking minute—who you saw, what you took, everything. And if you don't, I'm gonna see to it you go to jail for twenty years, and then you'll *really* have something to write about, at least when your ass isn't too sore to sit down from getting hit in the seat every day of your miserable fucking life."

"All right," Bobby says after a couple of seconds. "In exchange for immunity *and* anonymity, I'll give you the twenty-five percent. But if you want screen credit, you've gotta show me you can actually write—that you're more than just a cop with a bunch of bullshit stories you like to trot out for the tourists over a couple of beers. And till you prove different, all you are is the dummy and I'm the guy with my hand up your ass making your lips move."

Dennis is suddenly very tired, so he just says okay.

Bobby fetches him the tape of Linda screwing Ramon then clobbering him over the head with the four-pound Alma, plus he admits having the affair with Linda so he could, as Dennis put it, get inside her head a little. He even tells Dennis about the meeting in Vee's lawyer's office and how it wasn't until after she told him to go fuck himself that he got the idea to frame her for the murder, but it was just to teach her a lesson. He was never really going to let her take the fall for it.

Then he warns Dennis about Vee. "You saw the tape of her and Ramon, you got yourself a chubby thinking about it, so you think you'll just grab a piece, see what all the excitement's about, then move on. But it doesn't work that way with Vee.

She's a world-class cunt. She'll fuck you, then she'll fuck you over, just like she fucked me over."

"I don't want to hear this," Dennis says, his eyes going cold.

Maybe because Bobby's pissed off that Dennis wants to fuck his wife, or maybe because he doesn't realize how close Dennis is to beating him bloody, Bobby can't help but disregard the cautionary.

"All I'm saying is, Vee's long-term career aspirations don't include raising a couple of snot-nosed kids in Northridge with some blue-collar cop who's scrounging around the fringes of show business. That's not exactly the springboard to stardom she's always envisioned for herself. So I'm just saying, save yourself the grief. And if you can't, this is me saying I told you so, in advance."

CHAPTER 28

LATER THAT MORNING, DENNIS CALLS LINDA PAULSON and asks her if she'd mind coming in to Hollywood Division for a quick conversation this afternoon, he's got a couple of questions he'd like to ask her about Ramon. Is it urgent, Linda probes, or can it wait? Dennis says he wouldn't characterize it as urgent, exactly, but he'd like to put this part of the case to bed, as it were, and move on, but he can't do that until he rechecks some of his facts against her statements.

There's a pause on the line, then: "Is this something I should be worrying about, Detective? Am I going to be needing an attorney?"

Dennis assures her there's nothing to worry about and that she won't be needing an attorney. Linda says she's never been in a police station before, it should be interesting. Dennis promises to give her the VIP tour, and she tells him she'll see him some-time after lunch.

A few minutes short of three o'clock, Linda ar-rives at Hollywood Division and, goddamnit, she's a looker. There are some women who peak in their late teens, early twenties, beauty-wise, before start-ing the long, slow descent to hell in a handbasket. And then there are the women like Linda Paulson, who, plastic surgery notwithstanding, get sexier and more beautiful the older they get. (I always tell my wife, If I ever get in trouble, it's not going to be with a tootsie. But that's another story.)

So even in Hollywood Division, whose cops have seen more than their share of good-looking babes, Linda Paulson is a head-turner.

Upstairs in the detective squad, Dennis intro-duces Linda to his partner, Lonnie, then escorts her into the TV room.

"I really appreciate you coming over on such short notice," Dennis tells her.

"It sounded important," Linda says, looking around at the ratty couch, the chairs, and the table sitting in the center of the room.

"The thing is," Dennis says, getting right to it, "when I asked you did you know Ramon, you said hardly at all."

"That's correct."

He checks his notes. "You said, let me see here . . . you said it would be fun to take some classes, stretch out your acting muscles."

"That's right."

"What you didn't say was you were stretching out more than your acting muscles with Ramon."

Suddenly Linda gets all frosty. "What are you implying, Detective?"

Dennis grabs the remote and hits the PLAY button. The TV screen illuminates with the image of Linda and Ramon fucking, along with the muffled sounds of their passion: the headboard banging rhythmically against the wall, like a shutter slamming against the window frame when the Santa Anas blow; her escalating moans of "oh yes, baby, oh yes, oh God"; the dull smack of their sweaty bodies as Ramon rams in and out of her.

Dennis has seen the tape enough times that he's way more interested in watching Linda than watching the tape, and he can't help but be impressed by the fact that she doesn't flinch or drop her eyes in shame. From her expression, you'd think she was watching herself on some television show she was starring in. Of course, when you think about it, that's pretty much what it is, though I doubt you'd catch this particular episode on Must See TV.

Dennis freezes the tape before Linda and Ramon get to the main event. "Where did you get that?" Linda asks quietly.

Dennis tells her Ramon was into taping his sexual adventures with a camera hidden inside the armoire facing the bed, which is not altogether a direct answer to her question but which, under the circumstances, goes unchallenged.

"Why am I not surprised?" she asks, and now that Dennis has her full attention, he hits PLAY again, and

Linda watches as their postcoital conversation turns ugly, then escalates to violent, then murderous. When it's done, Dennis turns off the VCR.

"I thought you said I wouldn't be needing an attorney," Linda says.

"You don't," Dennis tells her. "At least not yet. What you need is a friend."

"And I'm supposed to believe that's you." Which is rhetorical in tone but which Dennis chooses to answer literally.

"I'll let you be the judge of that after you hear me out. And if you still want a lawyer after I'm through, I won't try and talk you out of it."

Dennis lets Linda's perception of her suddenly altered world sink in for a few moments before making his pitch. "I'm a cop. I've seen a lot worse than that, believe me," he says, pointing at the TV. "Plus, I understand a little something about human nature, and I make no judgments about your lifestyle. I tell you this because I want you to believe me when I say that I like you. You're smart, you're great-looking, you got a sense of humor, plus I'm guessing that being married to Marv Paulson's not the easiest ride in the amusement park, I don't care how much money he's got. So all in all, I have no interest in seeing you take a fall for a murder that could be argued was self-defense. So the only issue here is, do you exercise your right to an attorney or do you give me a statement first?"

"And how is that to my benefit?" Linda asks.

"Okay. Let's say you get an attorney in here. He's going to shut you down. Then I'm not going to have any choice but to arrest you, at which point you go into the system. You get arraigned, it's splashed all over the tabloids and the TV, and until you make bail—assuming the judge sets bail— you're in county lockup. Jail. And the reason all this happens is—don't kid yourself—that's the way your lawyer wants it. He gets to charge you a big number. He gets to go in front of the cameras. He gets to argue the case in a packed courtroom. But in the meantime, he's not the one doing prison time if the jury convicts. And he's not the one who has to live with that videotape being seen in open court."

Suddenly Linda imagines Bobby sitting in court, watching the videotape of her and Ramon. The thought of him seeing it and walking out of the courtroom and out of her life makes her heartsick.

Dennis pours her a glass of water. "Now, here's an alternative scenario. You tell me what you and Ramon were arguing about. You tell me how things got violent. You tell me how you knew enough about Ramon to know that before he reinvented himself as a successful actor, he'd done prison time for assault and rape. You say how you were in fear for your life and were just trying to protect yourself. Then, once I have your statement, I go to the D.A. I tell him I think you're telling the truth, that you cooperated fully, and that instead of arresting and charging you, we ought to go before a grand jury, where there's a good chance they'll find no true bill. And in the meantime, after you give me your statement, you walk out of here and have your dinner at home instead of at Women's Corrections."

"What happens to the tape in your scenario?" Linda asks.

"Grand jury evidence is sealed. If there's no true bill, the tape never comes out. If they indict, you've got bigger problems to worry about."

Linda takes a deep breath. "Ramon was trying to extort a million dollars from me to start a production company, or he was going to tell my husband we were having an affair. I told him it wasn't going to happen. He actually picked up the phone to call Marv. That's when I slapped him. He hit me back, and when he came after me, I hit him with his own fucking trophy."

"Because you were in fear for your life," Dennis prompts.

"Yes."

"And when we enhance the audio portion of the tape, is it going to corroborate what you're telling me about Ramon trying to extort you?"

"Yes."

"Okay, Mrs. Paulson. Let's get a D.A. in here and write it up."

Linda smiles at him for the first time since walking into the room. "Don't you think after watching that tape together, you can call me Linda?"

CHAPTER 29

IN THE WAKE OF LINDA'S CONFESSION THAT SHE KILLED Ramon (in self-defense) and the D.A.'s office announcing it would present its case to the grand jury, there commences a media frenzy, which the absence of hard facts does nothing to suppress. If anything, the scarcity of information fuels a cascading mud slide of rumor, gossip, and innuendo, with all the print rags and TV gossip shows dangling serious bucks for any scraps of information.

Linda hires a top-gun criminal attorney named Arlen Gillis to spin the information that inevitably leaks out, and for two weeks it's a media circus, culminating in the main event, the secret grand jury hearing itself, which results, after due deliberation, in a finding of no true bill, just as Dennis had predicted.

Normally, that would have been the end of it.

Grand jury proceedings are held in secret, the transcripts are sealed, and in a finding of no true bill, the evidence is never revealed. The problem is, this isn't normal. This is the gorgeous wife of a Hollywood billionaire, accused of murdering her Latin playboy lover in his Hollywood Hills boudoir. I mean, come on. There's no way the press lets up on this one. Would you?

And through it all Bobby keeps his head down and works on his screenplay, happily lost in the Zone.

Time, or at least the perception of it, changes profoundly when you're in the Zone. For a writer, being in the Zone means that some creative force beyond your control is driving you to work obsessively, all day, sometimes all night, with no sense of the passage of time, until exhaustion literally forces you away from the computer. And then, even after you've walked away, your brain continues to fire. You don't hear much of what people are saying to you over the din of voices in your head clamoring to be heard. You fall asleep at night, or sometimes at dawn, listening to them, only to wake up a dozen times in mid-thought, as if sleep hasn't been any impediment at all to the creative process. You come out of the shower and, soaking wet, scribble notes on the pad you keep handy, just in case. Your brain is like LAX the day before Christmas, with ideas stacked up like incoming planes, circling, waiting to land, so another one can take its place in the rotation. For sheer long-term excitement, nothing beats it.

But then, as Bobby approaches the finish line of

what feels like the best thing he's ever written, two things happen: the first thing is, he forgets, at least for the time being, the Devil's pact he made with Dennis. The second thing is, he unexpectedly hits a wall. Suddenly the faucet slows to a trickle. What had been effortless is now painstaking. The process becomes labored, and time—which seemed not to exist in the Zone—now looms large and weighs heavy, and Bobby fears that the magic has deserted him.

While Bobby suddenly finds himself creatively stalled, Linda, without any ambivalence whatsoever, is letting time work its healing magic on her wounds. But just as things are beginning to settle down, the shit *really* hits the fan when a bootlegged videotape of Linda Paulson fucking Ramon Montevideo becomes the hottest item to make the Hollywood rounds since the tape of Pamela Anderson blowing her skanky husband, Tommy Lee, on that boat.

Within days, every player in town has either seen or heard about the tape of her and Ramon, and if you could rent it at Blockbuster, there'd be a line out to the sidewalk. What had practically become a dead campfire with a few barely glowing embers has now erupted once again into a roaring blaze.

Predictably, Marv Paulson (who could tolerate—hell, to a point even enjoy—the idea of his wife banging Ramon) can't abide the humiliation of knowing that every one of his cronies, every person he does business with, every woman he meets, or every whore he beats has seen the tape of his wife riding Ramon like a bare-assed bucking bronco.

So, given the givens, it doesn't come as any great shock to Bobby when Linda shows up at his house about forty-eight hours after the tape hits the street, as it were, a little shell-shocked but strangely excited.

"How are you doing?" Bobby asks.

"Aside from the fact that I'm embarrassed and angry and I don't understand why Dennis Farentino would do this to me, I'm doing okay."

"How do you know it was Dennis?"

"No one else had access to the tape."

"Ten other cops had access to it," Bobby tells her. "The D.A.'s office had access to it. The clerks who handle the evidence for the grand jury had access to it. Christ, your own lawyer had access. And any one of them could've sold it to the tabloids for a hundred thousand bucks."

"Tell me the truth," Linda says. "Did you see it?"

"No," Bobby says.

"Promise me you never will."

"I promise."

"I came over to tell you that Marv wants a divorce."

"Are you okay with that?" Bobby asks.

"I'm more than okay," she tells him as Bobby pours her a glass of wine. "The more important question is, are *you* okay?"

"What do you mean?"

"What I mean is, one day you're having this nice,

quiet affair with a married woman and the next day you suddenly find out, along with the rest of the world, that she killed her previous lover. And if that's not enough of a scandal, the hottest ticket in town turns out to be the videotape of the last time they had sex, climaxing, if you'll pardon the expression, in the killing itself."

"Hey." Bobby shrugs. "Nobody's perfect."

"And just when you're probably thinking how much better off you are with this woman out of your life, she shows up on your doorstep saying her husband kicked her out and asking if she can spend the night."

"Yes," Bobby says.

"Yes you're okay with it or yes I can spend the night?"

"Yes I'm okay with it, and yes you can spend the night."

"Thank you," Linda says, and for the first time since this whole goddamn mess exploded in her face, she starts to cry. Bobby takes her in his arms and holds her, letting her cry herself out, then takes her hand and leads her to the bedroom, where she lets him undress her.

"You're not going to kill *me*, are you?" he asks, which actually gets a smile out of her.

"Not unless you get a heart attack while I'm fucking your brains out," she teases him, and that's the last either of them has to say for a good long while.

Bobby survives the lovemaking, and after they've shared a glass of wine, he asks her what she's going to do next. She says first she's going to get a suite at the Bel Air Hotel. Then she's going to hire a killer divorce attorney. She pretty much knows what Marv is worth, and for all his faults, he's not cheap. Besides, given his dirty little secrets, she doesn't figure Marv's up for much of a fight. When the dust settles, she tells Bobby, she should wind up with a settlement well north of a hundred million dollars, which, if she's careful, she figures she can get by on. "At least," she says, "till I find myself another rich husband."

"Would you consider a poor one?" Bobby asks.

"I thought you'd never ask," Linda says, starting to cry again, this time from happiness.

Bobby couldn't have written it any better.

CHAPTER 30

EVERY HOLLYWOOD SCANDAL HAS A SHELF LIFE, AND even this one—a classic by anyone's measure— eventually burns itself out. And as Linda's life settles back into some semblance of relative anonymity, her newly acquired divorce attorney very quietly negotiates a rapid dissolution of her twelve-year marriage to Marv. In her wildest dreams, Linda could never have imagined that roughly twenty-two years after leaving Ohio to seek her fame and fortune, she's achieved, if not exactly fame, then at least some measure of notoriety. As for the fortune part of the program, I think anyone would agree that 180 million bucks, give or take, qualifies big-time.

As far as Bobby's screenplay is concerned, the faucet has turned back on, his creative juices are flowing freely once again, and, happily back in the

Zone, he works on his script around the clock, finally writing FADE OUT one night around nine o'clock.

Bobby hits the PRINT key on his computer, and as the pages start to spit out of the printer, the doorbell chimes.

When he opens the door, Dennis is there. "Hey," he says.

"Hey," Bobby says back, a little startled.

"Can I come in?"

"Oh yeah, sure, come on in. Let me get you a beer."

In the kitchen, Bobby pops the caps off a couple of Coronas and gives one to Dennis. "You're spooky," he says.

"How's that," Dennis says, swigging the cold beer.

"I just literally finished the script five minutes before you showed up. It's printing as we speak. It's like you're a fucking mind reader."

"I *am* a mind reader," Dennis says.

"Oh yeah?" Bobby asks. "What am I thinking right now?"

"You're thinking I don't know it was you who leaked that tape of Linda and Ramon to the street."

Bobby thinks, Fuck. This guy *is* Columbo. He tells you he's smarter than you think and you *still* forget it.

"I'm not saying I did put it out there," Bobby says, "but you gotta admit, just when it seemed like the whole thing was fizzling out—boom—all hell breaks loose, it's the hottest story in town all over again, and her fat slob husband dumps her. It's a great story twist."

"Yeah. You humiliated her, you busted up her marriage—"

"She hated that fat fuck."

"—and turned her into a whore in the eyes of the whole town, just for a better ending to your screenplay."

"Grow up, Dennis. She's not a whore. She's a divorcée with a hundred and eighty million dollars who a thousand guys would commit murder to get next to."

Dennis wipes the sweat off his beer bottle with a paper towel before chucking it into the trash. "Are you two getting serious?" he asks.

"What, have you been spying on us?"

"You haven't exactly been sneaking around."

"Are you fucking my wife?" Bobby asks.

"We've been spending some time together," Dennis admits.

"I figured," Bobby says, and it's an index of how serious he and Linda *are* getting that he's not particularly angry about it.

"How's the script?" Dennis asks.

"Walk this way," Bobby says, and does a passable Groucho stride all the way to his office, where the last couple of pages are sliding out of the printer.

There's a special thrill writers feel when they print out that first copy of a finished script. Years ago, before word processors, you'd send your stuff to an outfit called Barbara's Place, where professional typists would format your script and print as many copies as you needed. It would take days, though, before you got the pleasure of hefting your newly finished script in your hand. But these days, with computers, script programs, spell checks, and a high-speed printer, you can do it yourself in a fraction of the time. And when it comes out of the printer, it's like bread coming out of the oven.

Bobby takes the 118-page script and raps it on the desk a few times to even up the edges, then hands it to Dennis as if he were a new parent letting him hold the baby for a minute. "Feel that," Bobby says proudly.

"It's warm," Dennis says.

"No, baby, it's hot. That's what a million bucks feels like. I'm calling it *Hollywood*. It's a morality tale. It's got it all—themes, melodrama, humor, sex, offbeat characters, plot twists—it's the best thing I've ever written."

"I know the story," Dennis says. "Tell me how it ends."

"Every piece of the plot fits," Bobby says, "and since this is Hollywood, everybody lives happily ever after. The writer's ex-wife gets tried for murder and acquitted, and the publicity makes her career. The writer falls in love with the Linda Paulson character, and she divorces her fat, rich husband. The writer writes his screenplay and sells it for seven figures against five percent of adjusted gross, and his ex-wife stars in it. The movie's a huge fucking hit, the writer marries Linda Paulson, and everybody lives happily ever after."

"What about the cop?"

"You're in it big," Bobby says. "You break the

case, and even though the writer's ex-wife gets off, you're okay with it, partly because you have a chubby for her, but mostly because you've been there too many times. You only catch 'em, you don't cook 'em. So whichever way it goes, you shrug your shoulders and move on to the next one. And after the wife gets off and she tells you she understands you were only doing your job, and since she senses there's chemistry between you, maybe now that she's free and single, you could spend some time together. And you know what you say?"

"Something like 'I'd like that, except I'd always be thinking you killed your last lover. How do I know you won't kill me?' "

Bobby grins and shakes his head in genuine admiration. "I keep trying to be mad at you, Detective, but I can't. You're too fucking smart. Plus I like you too much."

"So that's the ending?" Dennis asks.

"That's it. The writer marries Marv's rich ex-wife, *his* ex-wife becomes a movie star, the cop is the classic stoic hero who soldiers on alone, and the kicker is, no one ever knows that it was really the Linda Paulson character who murdered her Latin lover."

"See," Dennis says, "that's why you're a hack writer. You go for the bullshit ending."

Stung, Bobby says, "Oh yeah? You're such an experienced creative genius, you tell *me* what's a better ending."

Dennis weighs the script in his hand like the counter guy at Art's Deli in Studio City holding aloft a freshly sliced half-pound of lox on a thin piece of wax paper. "*Every*one knows Linda Paulson murdered her Latin lover," he says. "That's no surprise. A better ending is, the cop *kills* the writer, takes the script, puts his own name on it, sells it for seven figures, then fucks the dead writer's wife in the nice cushy bed in the bedroom of the Hollywood house she inherits when her husband gets killed."

Bobby stares at him, dumbstruck.

Dennis grins. "What do you think?"

"Shit," Bobby says. "That *is* better."

"Plus which," Dennis says, "I'd change the title."

"What's wrong with the title?"

"It's not specific enough. If it were my script, I'd call it *Death by Hollywood* so people would know it's a murder mystery."

Bobby shakes his head. "Too obvious. But you're right about the ending. I'm gonna rewrite it and give you shared story credit."

"Fuck shared story credit," Dennis says, and pulls the cold .22 out of his jacket pocket he's always kept handy just in case.

CHAPTER 31

YOU READ THE NEWSPAPER EVERY DAY, RIGHT? ALL THE really horrible local stuff is in the Metro section. In the *L.A. Times,* the section is called, simply, "California." What they *ought* to call it, simply, is "Murder." It seems like 75 percent of the California section every day is devoted to murder. Here's a typical sampling: DOUBLE MURDER IN LONG BEACH ... ACTOR ALLEGEDLY OFFERED TEN THOUSAND DOLLARS TO STUNTMAN TO KILL WIFE ... STALKER KILLS EX-GIRLFRIEND AND PARENTS ... TWENTY PEOPLE KILLED IN THREE-WEEK PERIOD IN SOUTH CENTRAL L.A.; SLAYINGS IN L.A. COUNTY REACH 329.

I hate to admit it, but who gives a shit? Let's be honest. It's not about us. It's not about anybody we know. It's not even in our neighborhood. It's just numbers. You browse the murders like you browse the obits, scanning the names on the off chance you'll recognize one. What really gets your blood up is the fucking stock market.

IRATE AOL TIME WARNER SHAREHOLDER MURDERS BROKER.

Now, *there's* one you'd read with more than passing interest. But four Mexicans killed by the niece's lunatic estranged husband? As they say in New York, fuggedabowdit.

Okay. Now ask yourself this. What would it be like if you opened the paper and read about a murder committed half a block from your house? Different story, right? And what if the victim was someone you knew? Suddenly it's not just newspaper blah blah blah. It's in your kitchen, so to speak. It's still not you, but it's close enough to get your attention. You can identify. Half a block away—shit, it *could've* been me. Or my kids. Or my neighbor's kids.

I remember years ago how deeply disturbed my whole street was when one of our neighbors died in a commercial-aviation disaster. That's when it gets too close. It penetrates your space. It's not just a bunch of illiterate illegals butchering each other in southeast L.A.

I raise the subject to put into some context for you a set of events you couldn't honestly imagine yourself going through, let alone contemplate the real-world emotional consequences of.

Have you ever killed anyone? Do you have any idea what it's like to physically kill another human being? Think about it. Soldiers do it in wars. Cops do it on the streets. They're trained for it, society by and large gives them permission to do it, and it *still* fucks them up unless they're psychotic, in which case they don't understand what all the fuss is about. But *you're* not psychotic, and neither am I (though my kids like to call me Psycho Dad when I yell at them to get off their cell phones before they get brain cancer).

Imagine—really try to imagine—killing someone. What would it do to you psychologically? How many nights' sleep would you lose, obsessively thinking about it? How much therapy would you need before the sheer fact of taking another human being's life stopped haunting you every day of your life?

Now, consider what it would be like if your luck was such that you not only experienced the trauma of killing someone (a lover, let's say) but then, not long after, experienced the compounding trauma of discovering someone else murdered (another lover, for instance). You may as well book a room at Bellevue right now.

Anyway, that's what happens to Linda Paulson when she shows up at Bobby's house later that night, expecting a glass of wine and a cozy hour or two of lovemaking and instead finds a horribly grim crime scene being supervised by homicide detective Dennis Farentino, who tells her that by all appearances, it looks like it was a home-invasion-type robbery, probably junkies. The house was pretty well ransacked, cash and valuables are missing, including the telescope that was out on the deck, as well as Bobby's computer. Dennis tells Linda they found a cheap .22 semi-automatic in the bushes outside the house that will probably turn out to be the murder weapon.

Dennis doesn't let Linda see the body—"You don't need that picture in your head," he tells her.

Dennis says he's got to ask about her whereabouts this evening, even though he doesn't believe for a minute, based on the evidence, that she had anything to do with Bobby's death.

Slumping into a chair in Bobby's living room, still in shock, Linda says she was at a charity auction at the Beverly Hilton Hotel. "What do I do now?" she asks, suddenly welling up, and Dennis can't help but feel sorry for her, seeing the terrible lost look in her eyes.

There's not much Dennis can say to comfort her, but he does his best, telling her that over the last couple of months, as he and Bobby had gotten friendly, Bobby had told him how much he loved Linda.

"When that tape of me and Ramon was making the rounds," she says, "I told Bobby I thought maybe you'd leaked it, and Bobby said no way."

"He was right," Dennis says.

"You were always straight with me," she tells him. "I should've known better. Bobby did."

"I appreciate your telling me," Dennis says.

"He talked about you all the time," Linda says. "He felt like the two of you were becoming really close friends." And now she starts to cry, and Dennis takes her in his arms and soothes her.

"We *were* close," Dennis admits. "I loved the guy. I'm going to miss him a lot."

Finally, Linda says she'd better get going, and Dennis walks her out, past the uniforms and the crime-scene folks, to her Mercedes.

"Are you okay to drive?" Dennis asks. "I can have someone drive you."

"No, I'm all right," she says. "I'm a tough broad. I'll be okay." Then she kisses Dennis on the cheek and thanks him for taking care of her. "Will you stay in touch, let me know how the investigation's going?"

Dennis promises he will.

"When all this settles down," Linda says, "maybe we can spend a little time together. I'm not big on shrinks, and I think I'll have a lot I'll want to talk about with someone I can trust."

"I'd like that," Dennis says, and watches her pull away from the curb, past the black-and-whites with their blazing bright light bars, heading down toward Sunset Boulevard. Dennis figures she won't be back up this way again till hell freezes over.

CHAPTER 32

I DON'T MEAN TO SOUND CYNICAL, BUT IN HOLLYWOOD a funeral is often like a premiere. You may not have any compelling reason to be there, but you want to show up anyway, just so everyone knows you have the clout to get in. Plus, let's face it—any big Hollywood event is a networking opportunity. So even though in the course of twenty-odd years in the business Bobby had met and worked with and for a lot of people, there's no way he even remotely knew all of the five hundred or so people who showed up for his memorial at Hillside Jewish Cemetery off the 405 South. And you know why I'm not cynical about it, even though I know most of them didn't give a shit about Bobby? Because of his mother, Esthelle.

It's a terrible thing for a mother to outlive her child, particularly an only child, and Bobby's death left Esthelle without family. No husband, no son, alone in New York City. At least, for this one day, she could take solace in the illusion that her son had all these close friends—that he was somebody, that he'd made it, he'd had success, and he was loved and would be missed by all these people, who were in the most glamorous business in the world, show business.

And if that wasn't exactly the truth, so what? It was certainly a version of the truth, and in this life some version of the truth is a hell of a lot better than no truth at all, especially if you're a mother who's lost her only son. Would she be better off knowing her son was a boozed-out hack whose wife was cheating on him and who wound up being murdered by a cop for his intellectual property (you should pardon the expression)? I think not.

Anyway, after Rabbi Baumgarten (who I assure you never met Bobby Newman in his life) gives an appropriately solemn and totally generic eulogy, offering all the appropriate prayers for the occasion, he turns over the microphone, to those of us so moved, to make a few remarks in memory of Bobby.

I go first, and I keep it short. I basically say I loved Bobby in spite of himself. I say the entertainment business is a lousy, dysfunctional family, but it's the only one we've got. I offer my thanks to God that at least Bobby died happy, doing what he loved, which was writing. I reflect on the irony of Bobby, who spent his whole career writing about crime, dying by it, and the further irony that somewhere out there a junkie too stupid and fucked-up to know it has Bobby's computer full of great stories and wonderful ideas.

Under the category Best Performance by a Hypocrite, the next person to speak about Bobby—hold on to your hats—is none other than Jared Axelrod. He must have been a frustrated actor at some point in his career, because this asshole gets up, starts to speak, and busts out crying. For the next five minutes, he sobs his way through an incoherent eulogy about what a great writer Bobby was, what a great friend he was, how much he'll be missed, and how it'll be a snowy day in July before Axelrod forgets everything that Bobby meant to him. This from the guy who'd been fucking Bobby's wife cross-eyed in suite 512 at the Peninsula Hotel two or three times a week for almost a year.

Next up is Vee, who won't make eye contact with Axelrod as she passes him on her way up to the podium. She speaks truthfully (more or less), albeit lovingly, about Bobby. She admits they'd had their ups and downs and that at the time of Bobby's death they were estranged. But she also acknowledges how much they'd loved each other, how they'd forged a life together, and—most important—how her life will forever be enriched for having had Bobby in it. Which is, to say the least, an understatement, given that because he died prior to their divorce she inherited his entire estate (though, in all fairness, money never was what the marriage was all about).

That said, the house is worth around a million-six and Bobby's various and sundry other assets (including his Writers Guild life insurance policy, plus his pension) are good for an additional 3 million bucks or so, giving Vee a grand total of well over 4 million. Maybe not a fortune by lottery standards, but she's not throwing it back.

There's an old joke about the Jewish guy who's dying at home, surrounded by his three loving sons. As the end nears, the old guy says, "Call the rabbi. I want him to bless you before I die."

The sons call the rabbi, who hurries to the dying man's side. "Please, Rabbi," the old man says. "Bless my sons."

The rabbi asks the first son what his name is, and the son says it's Bernie. "What do you do for a living, Bernie?"

"I'm a furrier," Bernie says, and the rabbi confers the appropriate blessing on his family, his kids, and his business.

Then the rabbi says to the second son, "What's your name and what do you do?"

The second son says his name is Milton and he's an attorney. The rabbi blesses his family, his kids, and his practice.

Finally, the rabbi says to the third son, "And what's your name?"

The third son says, "My name is Sol."

"And what do you do for a living, Sol?" asks the rabbi.

"I'm a Broadway talent scout," Sol says, and the rabbi belts out the first sixteen bars to "Some Enchanted Evening."

I tell you this joke by way of what I hope is some partial explanation for what Bobby's mother did when she got up to the podium to eulogize her son after Vee was finished speaking.

Esthelle is a little, silver-haired, belligerent woman with a biting wit who did battle all her life with anyone who'd stand still long enough to take the beating.

At the podium, her head barely poking up over the top, she takes a moment to look out over the SRO crowd.

"My son Bobby's death reminds me of an old joke," she finally says. "The great Jewish actor Moscowitz collapses onstage in the middle of a performance of *King Lear*. After about twenty minutes, the stage manager comes out and says to the audience, 'I'm sorry to inform you that Mr. Moscowitz has died.' From the second balcony, a voice calls out, 'Give him an enema!' The stage manager looks up, annoyed, and says, 'You don't understand. The Yiddish Theater has lost one of its greatest artists.' Again, from the second balcony, 'Give him an enema!' 'Sir,' the stage manager says, 'Moscowitz is *dead*. It won't help.' And from the second balcony, the voice calls back, 'It couldn't hurt.' "

Silence. People are stunned. Then there are a few titters here and there as Bobby's mom just stands there gazing out at the audience. And finally, as the titters give way to laughter and the laughter becomes a rolling, unstoppable avalanche, the place is up for grabs.

If you ever wondered why those idiots go on the Ricki Lake or the Jerry Springer shows to spill their worst, pathetic secrets to a predatory, contemptuous viewing public, there's your answer: just like everybody else, it seems, Bobby's mom wanted her fifteen minutes of fame.

And you wonder how come Bobby wound up in show business.

You'd think that would be the end right there. But you'd be wrong. When the laughter finally begins to subside, Linda Paulson gets up and approaches the podium. If you don't think that quiets the room in a hurry, guess again.

Eyes wet with emotion but voice strong, Linda says, "In case most of you don't recognize me with my clothes on, my name is Linda Paulson." If you thought it was quiet before, now you can hear the proverbial pin drop. "You all think you've seen me naked. You haven't. You may have seen my body, and shame on you if you did, but Bobby Newman is the only man who ever truly saw me naked. He was the only man I ever really trusted or loved. He made me feel wanted, he made me feel smart, he made me feel like there really was something worth living for, and when he made love to me, I understood what it meant to be happy. I'm sorry he's gone. I'll miss him for the rest of my life. But I'll always be grateful for having had him in my life the short time I did, because he gave me back something I thought I'd lost forever—my self-respect. God bless you, Bobby."

And that, finally, was the funeral.

CHAPTER 33

I'M SITTING IN MY OFFICE ONE MORNING A FEW DAYS after the funeral, leafing through the day's editions of *Variety* and *The Hollywood Reporter*. In the middle pages of each publication is a simple memorial ad dedicated to Bobby that reads IN LOVING MEMORY OF BOBBY NEWMAN. I'LL MISS YOU ALWAYS under a picture of him.

I've never understood those ads. First of all, the guy's dead, so he isn't going to see the ad or appreciate the sentiments of its author. Second, it seems to me that the ad is really more about the person buying it than it is about memorializing the deceased. It's as if the person is saying that his love is so fucking special, so entirely more important than *your* love, that he has to buy an ad in the trades to let you know about it. Plus, it's like pissing five thousand bucks down a sinkhole. Why not donate the money to charity instead, in the dearly departed's name?

Anyway, I'm sitting there curdling into a complete cynic right before my very own eyes when Dennis Farentino calls. We'd sat next to each other at the funeral, and when it was over, he'd said he'd like to call me in a few days if that was all right, and I'd said of course. Over the phone, he asks if we can get together for lunch sometime, so I suggest the Grill. He says when, I say today if you'd like, and that's how my relationship with Dennis gets started.

I've met, and known, a lot of famous people over the years, and I'm pretty used to it. It takes a lot for me to be starstruck, though I must admit I can get a little tongue-tied around famous athletes. I love sports, and it's not my end of the business, so on the rare occasions when I do meet a sports star, I begin to get a sense of how the average person must feel when he or she sees Brad Pitt in a restaurant and just has to ask him for his autograph, forget about the fact he's eating his dinner or in the middle of a business meeting. (Asking for autographs being another thing I don't get. I remember once stepping into an elevator that Shaquille O'Neill was in. Seven feet tall, 350 pounds is big anywhere, but in an elevator, it's absolutely *huge*. Plus, he's one of my all-time sports idols, I had him captive, and it *still* didn't occur to me to bug him for an autograph. I sort of nodded, he sort of grunted, and the ten-second elevator ride was one of the longest of my life.)

Anyway, the point being that while meeting

celebrities is, by and large, run of the mill for me, there's something about meeting cops that I think most people (myself included) are very impressed by. Maybe it's the simple fact that they're wearing a gun as casually as you're wearing a necktie. Or maybe it's how safe being with a cop makes you feel, which is always a surprise, because you're never really conscious of how *un*safe you feel most of the time. Or maybe it's just that they know stuff—secrets—that most of us don't know and your personal relationship puts you privy to it. Like, for instance, what Dennis told me about Daniel Deveaux.

Daniel Deveaux is two things, and you might remember him for both: he's an actor and he's an asshole. He was also a pretty big television star for about twenty minutes, and I represented him (for about that same twenty minutes).

Daniel (God forbid you called him Dan or Danny; that would buy you a five-minute harangue) had been knocking around for years, getting small parts here and there, but never really breaking through. He was in his mid-thirties, not particularly good-looking in any traditional sense, but he had a certain quality that was appealing nevertheless. Plus, it didn't hurt that he was talented; I'll give him that.

Anyway, Daniel finally lands the big one—a lead role in a new TV series, and no question, it's the biggest break of his life. The reviews are great, the ratings are strong, and Daniel is the new flavor of the month. Every actor's dream, right? By all measures, his career is ready to rocket into orbit. So what happens? This idiot decides he's too big for television. He wants to be a movie star. He develops a serious attitude problem. He constantly denigrates the material ("Who writes this shit?" was a particularly galling quote recollected by the writing staff). He alienates his fellow cast members. When everyone should be enjoying the miracle of a successful new show, this jerk is poisoning the well.

One time, he punched out an associate producer, then locked himself in his trailer, refusing to come out till they sent for his shrink. The production manager got in touch with the doctor, who came right over, huddling with Daniel for half an hour in his trailer.

When the shrink finally came out, he said to the production manager, "Why don't you take an early lunch break, and when you're done, Daniel will go back to work."

The production manager said okay, sure, what choice have we got anyway, and as the shrink was leaving, the guy said, "Doc, before you go, can you tell me what's his problem?"

The shrink stopped, turned back to the guy, and said, "What's his problem? He's *crazy,* that's his problem."

And I'm in the middle of this shit storm. The producers are calling me to complain about Daniel, Daniel is calling me to complain about the producers, every movie studio in town is calling with offers of starring roles during the show's hiatus, and the general tension surrounding this guy's new-found fame is excruciating.

Somehow everyone survives the first season, and during the summer hiatus, with Daniel off making a movie in New York, the show is nominated for a couple of dozen Emmy Awards, including one for Daniel as Best Actor. Fat city, right? Fat chance is more like it.

Now he wants out of his contract so he can pursue his long-held dream of movie stardom. I point out to him that it makes no sense. I can get him a hefty raise. He can solidify his position as a star. He can make movies during the off-season. Look at Ted Danson, I say. Look at Alan Alda. (If *E.R.* had been around then, I would have said, Look at George Clooney.) All these guys are huge television stars, they make millions of bucks, plus they do movies, and every-body they work with loves them. How bad is that?

Nothing doing. Daniel wants out. I try to explain to him the consequences of his actions. They can sue him. Or they might retaliate by reducing his role to a glorified extra—believe me, I've seen it happen. Finally, as a cautionary tale, I invoke the two magic words: Pernell Roberts.

Pernell Roberts was one of the original three sons in the television series *Bonanza,* along with Michael Landon and Dan Blocker. Pernell decides after a couple of seasons that he's too big for televi-sion, and wants out of his deal to pursue a movie career. They finally release him, *Bonanza* runs about seventeen years, everyone becomes really rich and really famous (and, of course, in Blocker's case, really dead), and Pernell Roberts's career, for all intents and purposes, goes in the toilet.

Anyhow, to make a long story short, Daniel remains adamant. And, of course, by now there's also a manager in the picture, along with a big-shot entertainment attorney. So the three of us, including some punk associate the attorney drags along so he can bill an extra two hundred an hour, all troop over to the executive producer's office for a Big Meeting.

To be perfectly honest, I was against it from the beginning. I thought Daniel ought to be thanking his lucky stars he had a fucking job, for Christ's sake, instead of trying to weasel out of his contract, but hey—this is Hollywood. Everyone signs off on the contract knowing that in success there basically *is* no contract, that the actor has you by the balls, and if he (or she) is willing to be a complete shit and stay home, there's really not a goddamn thing you can do about it except give them the fucking raise. This is America, baby. Fuck the contract.

Anyway, there we all are in the executive producer's office, for one of the most uncomfortable meetings I've ever attended in my life. The room is jammed. There's the executive producer, of course, along with the president of the production company (also a lawyer, by the way), plus the production company's business-affairs guy (another lawyer), and with all those lawyers in one room, it won't come as a big shock when I tell you that the meeting gets testy almost immediately.

First, the manager says Daniel feels he's been persecuted all year; that because of his script complaints, the writers have reduced the size of his role. The executive producer says that's bullshit. Everyone—the public, the media, the producers themselves—acknowledge he's the star.

Then the president of the company cuts to the chase, wanting to know what Daniel's looking for. The lawyer, trying to hide the smirk on his face, says, "Our demands are based on the theory of diminished opportunity."

"What the fuck is that?" asks the executive producer, and I can tell already this guy's not gonna last the whole meeting before blowing out his carotid.

"Diminished opportunity," the lawyer explains, "goes like this. Daniel is currently in New York making a movie for seventy-five thousand dollars a week. Coming back to the series for a second season at the contractual rate of forty-two-five an episode represents a big pay cut—hence, a diminished opportunity."

Now the executive producer starts to squirm around in his chair, he's so pissed off. "Let me tell you my theory of *enhanced* opportunity, counselor, which holds that if not for the success of this series, your idiot client wouldn't be in New York making seventy-five thousand a week in the first place!"

"That may be true," says the lawyer, "but that was then and this is now." In other words: this is a stickup; reach for the sky.

Now, I'm an agent. My job is to get the best deal

I can for my client, and I like to think I'm not incapable of playing hardball when the occasion calls for it. But this has me squirming in my seat, too.

Finally, the president of the company, who happens to be the only female in the room, and a goddamn good-looking one at that, says, "What is it exactly you're looking for?"

Straight-faced, the lawyer ticks it off on his fingers: one, a hundred thousand dollars per episode. Two, Fridays off. Three, a thirty-eight-foot trailer. Four, an office on the lot. Five, a development executive of his own, to be paid (by the production company) a thousand dollars a week. Six, two hotel suites in New York when the company's on location. Seven, a dozen first-class plane tickets. Plus, eight, additional security to shield this clown from his adoring public. By now, the lawyer's running out of fingers. It's like the twelve fucking days of Christmas.

The executive producer laughs out loud. "You've got to be kidding," he says.

Unfazed, the lawyer comes back with plan B. "If you're not willing to meet the first set of demands," he says, "there's a second set of demands that would not make Daniel *as* happy but that he's willing to live with." And then he starts with the fingers again.

"Sixty-five thousand per episode, Fridays off, the office, the development executive, the tickets, the suites, the trailer, and, last but not least, the final seven episodes off so he can have a larger window of opportunity for doing feature films during the hiatus."

The executive producer is shaking his head in disbelief. Can you imagine letting the star of your show take a leave of absence for fully one third (and the final third at that) of the season?

"And, lastly," the lawyer states, "if neither of the two options is acceptable, the third option is to release him from any further obligation to the series so he can pursue his feature film career full-time."

By now the executive producer looks like he's ready to throw a punch. He's red in the face, and the veins are sticking out on his neck. "How about this," he proposes. "Your fucking client has a contract, we've exercised his option for a second year at forty-two-five an episode, and if he doesn't report for work on August eighth, we'll sue his ass for breach of contract."

Needless to say, that was the end of the meeting. I won't bore you with the rest of the story, which you can probably figure out anyway.

Pernell Roberts ring a bell?

There's another story about Daniel Deveaux, which is where Dennis comes in. Before he became a TV star (for the aforementioned twenty minutes), Daniel was having an affair with this actress named Wendy Marx, who was also a highly regarded acting teacher. Like Ramon Montevideo almost twenty years later, Wendy had a habit of taking her students as lovers, and Daniel was her hump *du jour*.

One night after class, Daniel and Wendy were confronted by a gun-toting junkie in the parking lot adjacent to the building she taught in, and tragically, Wendy was shot and killed. Dennis Farentino, then a young homicide detective, caught the case.

The local publicity from the case was considerable and actually brought Daniel to the attention of the director who finally cast him in the TV series that made him a star, so in a sense you could say Daniel Deveaux turned a lemon into lemonade, big-time.

Dennis tells me over lunch that when they finally caught the kid who killed Wendy Marx, he said the shooting was an accident; that instead of just forking over his wallet, Deveaux was trying to be a hero, and in the ensuing struggle, the gun went off and Wendy was killed instantly.

So this asshole Deveaux not only was responsible for Wendy's death but he used the publicity from it to parlay himself into a career. I suppose the fact that, being an asshole, he finally parlayed himself *out* of a career qualifies as ironic justice, of sorts.

During that period of time before Deveaux imploded, however, he befriended Dennis, who'd never actually gotten close to a celebrity before, and they spent a fair amount of time drinking and gambling and womanizing together. Dennis provided Daniel with a degree of personal security he wasn't used to but quickly learned to enjoy (and take advantage of), and Daniel gave Dennis an entrée to Hollywood he'd never enjoyed before. This is called symbiosis, kids, and Dennis and Daniel, pretty much the same age, were a mile up each other's ass.

Which is why, when Daniel hit the bookies for six

hundred thousand dollars, Dennis, against his better judgment, went to New York City to pick up the
money for him.

In any event, by the time we've gone back and
forth with our Daniel Deveaux stories, Dennis and
I have hit it off pretty well, and he finally asks me if
I know what Bobby was working on when he died.

"No," I say. "He wouldn't tell me. He said he
wanted to finish it and have me read it cold. He was
pretty excited, though."

"Did he say anything about the project *we* were
working on?"

Again I tell him no, so Dennis explains that it was
an idea for a cop show he wanted to call *Blind Justice,* which he says he told Bobby with the notion
that Dennis would provide the stories and Bobby'd
write it, but now that Bobby's gone, Dennis is
thinking maybe he'd like to pitch it to HBO himself, and would I be interested in representing him,
since Bobby always spoke so highly of me.

No one's immune to flattery or the prospect of
earning a buck, so I tell Dennis I'd be delighted to
represent him, but who's going to do the actual
writing?

"I was thinking," Dennis says sheepishly, "I'd
take a shot at it myself. Bobby said I was a natural
storyteller, and if I could tell a story I could write it,
so I'm thinking, Why not? I mean, who knows more
about this stuff than me anyway? In fact," he goes
on to say, "I was thinking there might also be a really good movie in this Ramon Montevideo case."

"Well," I say, not wanting to burst his bubble, "no one knows the story better than you."

"I'm thinking I might take a whack at it," Dennis says. "I've never actually had the balls to try it, but I think it might be fun."

I don't want to piss all over Dennis's fantasy, but it's not too often a cop suddenly turns in his badge to become a successful writer, Joe Wambaugh notwithstanding.

"I know it sounds pretty naïve," Dennis says, reading my mind, "and it's probably a lot harder than it looks, but what the hell. If I really stink up the joint, I can always count on you to tell me, right?"

"I promise if you stink up the joint, I'll tell you," I say, and Dennis's smile is heartbreakingly sad.

"Y'know, Bobby's death hit me hard," he says. "I hadn't made a friend in a long time, and suddenly here's this guy in my life I can really talk to about stuff. Most of the guys I know, if we argue, it's about where to go for dinner. But Bobby and I, we had *real* arguments. He gave me the idea I could be something more than a cop. I guess I want to try and honor that idea."

Suddenly there's a lump in Dennis's throat and he's wiping his eyes and apologizing. "I'm sorry. But I miss him."

In all honesty, I do too, and I puddle up a little myself.

CHAPTER 34

OVER THE COURSE OF THE NEXT THREE MONTHS OR SO, Dennis calls me once or twice a week, just to check in and report on his progress. With Bobby as his inspiration, he says, he's writing every night after work, and by the time the three months have gone by, he's written an entire screenplay, called *Death by Hollywood*, which, as advertised, is about the murder of Ramon Montevideo. But it's more than just a murder mystery, Dennis says. It's also a tribute to Bobby, who's the central character in the movie.

I can tell you now that when I read the script, I was shocked at how good it was and by how much of it was infused with Bobby's style and sensibility, almost as if his spirit had been watching over Dennis as he wrote. It gave me chills reading it.

That I didn't realize the title page should have

read "*Stolen* by Dennis Farentino" instead of "Written by" him is an index, I suppose, of how naïve and gullible I am. It simply never occurred to me, until later, that Dennis was passing off Bobby's last script as his own. And even when that idea did take hold of me, the thought that Dennis might have actually *murdered* Bobby for his computer was inconceivable. But I'm getting ahead of myself.

One week after I read *Death by Hollywood,* Dennis and I are sitting in Jared Axelrod's office, along with his tight-assed little development executive, Lainie Ginsberg, and he's raving about the script. He says it's one of the best screenplays he's ever read. "It's got everything. Great story, lots of sex, and I love the dark humor," he says, raising his hands above his head like a referee, palms facing each other. "It's a fucking touchdown." He says he can see Mel Gibson, or maybe Brad Pitt, as the cop, and Kevin Spacey would be perfect as the writer. "And how about *Mrs.* Brad Pitt for the part of the writer's wife?" And he raises his hands again, shouting, "Touchdown!"

As much as I'm thinking, What an asshole, I'm also thinking, What a payday.

"So, Jared," I say, looking to close, "what kind of deal are we talking about?"

"Well," he says, fucking weasel that he is, "it *is* a first screenplay."

Dennis gets up from the couch and extends his hand to Axelrod. "Nice talking to you, Jared," he says. Then, to me, "Come on, Eddie. Let's go."

"Hold it, hold it, hold it," Axelrod says. "Let me finish. It's the *best* first screenplay I've ever read, and I'm prepared to offer you a preemptive bid of one million dollars."

Dennis sits back down.

"We've already turned down a million two-five against five percent of adjusted gross from Paramount," I lie.

"All right, you've got a gun to my head. I love this script, I want this script," Axelrod whines. "I'll give you one point five against seven adjusted."

"I tell you what," Dennis says before I can respond. "I don't know anything about how your business works, so it's not that I don't trust you guys, but how about you keep the back end, make it two million cash, and she's all yours?"

Axelrod's hands signal touchdown again. "Deal." And just like that, Dennis has sold his script for two million dollars, and because Hollywood producers are essentially junkies always looking to score, Axelrod says, "As long as we're all here, what else have you got in your back pocket?"

Dennis says, "I've got an idea for a TV series I'm calling *Blind Justice,* about a cop who loses his eyesight in a shootout but stays on the job."

"I love it," Axelrod says. "But why not make it a movie first, then do the series?"

"Hey," Dennis says, grinning. "You're the expert. I'm just the writer."

And we walk out of Axelrod's office with *two* deals. When we walked in, Dennis was a cop making eighty-five grand a year. When he walked out, he was a multimillionaire.

Puts a different spin on the whole concept of identity theft, doesn't it?

On the way out of Axelrod's office, Dennis stops and tins Sylvia, the hatchet-faced assistant. "Sylvia," he says, "you're under arrest for felony impersonation of a human being. You have the right to remain silent. You have the right to an attorney. Anything you say can and will be used against you in a court of law."

Then he gives her his impish grin, and because Dennis has suddenly become a star, the old bitch actually smiles, charmed, and I have to vacate the area quickly so as not to laugh out loud.

CHAPTER 35

THAT NIGHT, DENNIS AND VEE CELEBRATE DENNIS'S newfound success with dinner at Spago, in Beverly Hills, after which they go back to her house and make love in the nice cushy king-size bed that used to belong to her and Bobby.

And after, because it's an unusually warm night for this time of year, they take their refilled champagne glasses and walk naked out onto the deck to look at the bright, twinkling lights of Hollywood. Vee says to Dennis that she never knew it could be like this, that Dennis is the first man she could ever see spending the rest of her life with. And Dennis, thinking his own feelings for Vee might be moving in the same direction, is smart enough to keep his mouth shut. He takes her in his arms and kisses her, she kisses him back, and after a couple of minutes of serious tonsil hockey, Vee slides down between Dennis's legs and commences giving him the oral B-plus special, right out there on the deck, with the HOLLYWOOD sign in the distance.

CHAPTER 36

THREE DAYS LATER, DENNIS AND I ARE SITTING IN BRIAN Grazer's office. Brian's a character. Small and wiry, with goofy, gel-spiked hair, it's easy to think he's some kind of hyperkinetic adolescent with the attention span of a six-year-old. But if you did think that, you would be very wrong. In fact, he's an extremely smart, very astute producer who, like Dennis, likes to lull you into a false sense of superiority. And if you fall for it, he'll probably wind up having you for lunch. Trust me when I tell you it's not luck that's put a string of box office hits as long as your arm on his résumé. This is a guy who's done everything from *The Grinch Who Stole Christmas* to *A Beautiful Mind*. It's no accident that there's an Oscar in his trophy case.

Anyway, we're sitting in Brian's office in a Wilshire Boulevard high-rise right around the cor-

ner from the Grill, because Dennis has an idea he
wants to pitch. And because Brian's heard about
Axelrod buying the *Death by Hollywood* script,
not to mention the deal for *Blind Justice,* he's extremely gracious toward Dennis, who, in his best
Columbo way, tells him that he has a nine-year-old
nephew named Mikey and the Grinch movie is his
all-time favorite, he watches it over and over, so
when Dennis had this idea for an animated kids'
movie, he immediately thought of Brian.

Now, Brian's like a kid himself, practically levi-
tating out of his chair. "Tell it to me, I want to hear
it," he says, and Dennis can't help grinning at
Brian's infectious enthusiasm.

"Okay," Dennis starts. "The movie's called *First
Dog,* and it's about this talking dog named Bob,
who becomes president of the United States . . ."
And because Brian's already captured by the
thought of it, neither he nor Dennis can see the
color draining out of my face.

CHAPTER 37

BEING A SUCCESSFUL AGENT IN HOLLYWOOD REQUIRES a kind of willful ignorance. I know I've preached the virtues of telling the truth, but by the same token, I don't necessarily believe the truth will set you free. I've seen too many examples in this town of the truth actually getting you killed, figuratively speaking anyway. So in the neutral zone that exists between not lying but not always exactly telling the truth, there lurks the Clinton doctrine as it applies to gays in the military: don't ask, don't tell. In other words, go along to get along.

I guess it was Bobby's murder that dragged me, kicking and screaming as it were, to a place where I realized I couldn't just go along anymore. I had to confront Dennis, knowing full well that we were two voyagers passing in opposite directions. Dennis was in a rudderless ship on a journey away from his moral center, and I was setting sail from the land of situational ethics toward an island of absolute moral conviction. And I was realizing as well, with equal parts fear and excitement, that my boat was also rudderless, its course irrevocably set. Having belatedly blundered into what I hoped was my own true moral nature, it took me about the length of time it takes to get to the parking garage under Brian Grazer's building to realize that if I didn't finally look Dennis in the eye and tell him I knew what he'd done, I wouldn't be able to look *myself* in the eye.

It was a pretty scary decision, particularly if what I was suddenly starting to believe was actually true—namely, that Dennis had gone up to Bobby's house, murdered him, and made it look like a junkie had broken in and stolen a bunch of his shit, including his computer.

The fact that he had Bobby's computer and had stolen his scripts and stories was, as far as I was concerned, indisputable. What was up for grabs, of course, was whether Dennis had killed him for it.

At the car, Dennis looks at me, knowing I'm chewing on something. "You haven't said a word since we left his office. What's going on?"

I take a deep breath and start. I tell him I wasn't sure about the script, that it sounded like Bobby's voice, but I couldn't be sure, and there was certainly no way to prove he'd written it. Plus, I admit, I was seduced, not only by the high price the script fetched but by the sudden heat my new client, the next Joseph Wambaugh, was generating. Then, while the *Blind Justice* idea seemed vaguely familiar, I couldn't really place it. And so it wasn't until he pitched *First Dog* to Brian Grazer that I was positive. "I read that story five years ago," I tell Dennis. "But it took me a while to put it together. I knew *Blind Justice* was familiar, I just couldn't think why, but that was in the story too, about the writer with the talking dog who gives him a bunch of ideas, and one of them turns into a smash-hit TV series."

Dennis says that Bobby told him no one had ever read it. I tell him I'm not no one—I'm his agent, for Christ's sake, I read *everything*. And probably because I told him I didn't think it was very commercial, he never showed it to anyone else.

Unfazed, Dennis says that Bobby had let him read the story when they first began talking about collaborating, and both ideas had kind of stuck in his head. "Besides, with Bobby dead, what's the difference?"

"The difference," I say, "is that any way you slice it, you stole another writer's ideas and represented them as your own, and in all good conscience I feel that it's probably best for all concerned if we part company."

"I think it's a mistake to fire me," Dennis says, suddenly cold-eyed, and I imagine the coldness of those blue eyes being the last thing Bobby registered before Dennis shot him with that .22.

"Your secret's safe with me," I say. "I just can't represent you, knowing what I know."

"You don't *know* anything," Dennis says.

"I know you stole his work," I tell him. "What I don't know is whether you murdered him for it. Not that I could ever prove it anyway—you're too good for that."

"Then for the sake of argument," Dennis says, "let's pretend I did what you think I did. If you can't prove it, why not just continue to represent me and make a pile of money?"

"Agents may not be the most ethical people in the world," I say, "but Bobby wasn't just a client. He was a friend. And if I turn my back on that, I'm no better than you are."

"So under the circumstances," Dennis says, "I guess a blow job is out of the question."

And if I hadn't been so scared, I probably would have laughed . . .

CHAPTER 38

WOULDN'T BLAME YOU IF YOU'VE GOTTEN THE IMPRES-
sion that I have a somewhat cynical view of the
entertainment business. But you know what they
say: cynicism is idealism betrayed. And while I admit my worldview has been somewhat jaundiced
by experience, I want to also make it clear (for
whatever it's worth) how much I love the business.
At its best, it's magical, artful, and thrilling. Making a great movie or television series really *is* like
catching lightning in a bottle. Even when it happens, you're not quite sure how, but you know that
somehow a group of artists and craftsmen came together to create something which, at its best, is
greater than the sum of its parts. And if you've ever
experienced it, you know that it's the best feeling in
the world. You've *created* something, or at least
been a part of something, that has brought plea-

sure, laughs, tears, and insights to a mass audience. You've touched people's lives, and it doesn't get any better than that.

Which is why there was a time, in my early teens, when I entertained the notion of becoming a writer. I'd read somewhere that Thomas Wolfe used to write *You Can't Go Home Again* in longhand on legal tablets, standing in front of his refrigerator, using its top as a writing surface. What an image. This tall man, writing all night and into the wee hours of the morning, alone in his kitchen, penning the great American novel. It's the stuff of fantasy, and whenever I imagined myself as a writer, that was the image my brain conjured. The only problems being, I wasn't tall enough and I wasn't good enough.

Nevertheless, like every aspiring young writer, the idea of writing a novel is what it was all about for me. So it's ironic that all these years later I've written what amounts to a novel-length manuscript that reads like the stuff of fiction. Except it's not.

While I obviously made up a lot of the dialogue between the principals in the story, I did so based on extensive conversations I had over the course of the last six months with Vee, Linda, Dennis, and of course Bobby himself, before he died. And when you do the math, it all adds up as neatly as two plus two.

I'm convinced Bobby saw Linda kill Ramon. He says as much in his screenplay (the one with Dennis's name on it). I'm also convinced Bobby sneaked into Ramon's house and stole the tapes of Vee and Linda having sex with him.

I believe Bobby insinuated himself into Linda's

and Dennis's lives so that he could write his screenplay with the kind of realism that only comes from
firsthand knowledge of their psyches. What I don't
think Bobby anticipated was the extent to which
he'd become so emotionally involved with them.
But that's what good writers do. They go places
most of us are afraid to go.

I also believe Bobby framed Vee in a drunken,
jealous rage, and I believe that when Dennis finally
figured out the puzzle, he made the decision that ul-
timately cost Bobby his life.

There's this old joke about the unsuccessful Hollywood hack who wakes up one morning to find a
mysteriously uncredited script sitting on top of his
typewriter. It's a brilliant piece of work, and the
writer puts his name on it without hesitation and
sells it for a bunch of money. About a month later,
another script materializes, and he sells that one for
even more. Half a dozen scripts later, the writer is
living large in Bel Air, he has gorgeous women at
his beck and call, and more money than he knows
what to do with.

One night he hears tapping noises coming from
his office and sneaks down to take a look. There, at
his typewriter, is this ugly little troll, typing away.

"*You're* the one responsible for all those scripts,"
the writer says with awe, and the troll sheepishly
admits as much.

"My God," the writer says. "I owe you everything. I have success beyond measure. I have
money, women, this beautiful house, and all because of you."

The troll nods, embarrassed, and the writer says, "You've got to let me thank you properly. What do you want? I'll give you anything. Money. Women. Cars. Name it."

The troll says he has no interest in any of these things but perhaps the writer might consider, just this once, letting the troll share screen credit on this script he's just finishing.

The writer looks at the troll, stunned. "*Screen* credit? Fuck *you*, screen credit!"

I mention this joke because it's illustrative of what happened to Bobby. First, Dennis figures out what Bobby's done and uses it to blackmail Bobby into forking over a piece of the action. And then, when Bobby finally offers Dennis shared screen credit, Dennis essentially says, Fuck *you*, shared screen credit, and kills the poor bastard so he can steal the whole ball of wax.

I never would have figured any of this out if Dennis hadn't gotten greedy and pitched that talking-dog story to Brian Grazer. Once he did, though, all the pieces fell into place. Like I told Dennis, I'll never be able to prove it, but I'm a little nervous anyway. Actually, if you want to know the *absolute truth*, I'm more than a little nervous. I'm actually pretty goddamn scared.

Think about it. Maybe I can't prove Dennis killed Bobby, but I can sure as hell burst his bubble. Gossip and innuendo being what they are in this town, I could probably put some serious stink on him. Plus, I know Vee—she'd drop him like a hot rock.

If I were a naturally suspicious type like Dennis, I

don't know how comfortable I'd be knowing there was someone in my life who could hang me out to dry, which is why I've written this manuscript. It took me four months, and I'm not even proofing it as I go, since I have no intention of ever showing it to anybody. Along with the copy of Bobby's story "First Dog," which I dug out of my files, it's going directly into my safe-deposit box at City National Bank—an insurance policy, if you will—just in case Dennis ever tries to threaten or intimidate me. The irony is, I not only loved writing it, I also think it's pretty good. Maybe even as good as Bobby's screenplay, which Dennis got two million bucks for.

Nevertheless, the only possible way I can imagine anyone ever reading this thing is if I died. And if that were to happen anywhere in the near term, you can bet your house it'd be because Dennis actually got worried enough to kill me.

I want to thank my dear and gifted friend David Milch for urging me to write this novel. I'd also like to thank another great friend and collaborator, Alison Cross, for seconding the motion. My heartfelt thanks as well to Bill Clark, whose life and whose friendship have informed this book.

I want to express in particular my gratitude to my friend Fred Specktor, whose constant enthusiasm, encouragement, and advice inspired me.

My thanks to Mort Janklow for representing my efforts with such talent, regard, and affection, and for warning me about the siren's call of novel writing.

"When you write novels," Mr. Janklow told me, "your office is always in your head." Boy, was he ever right.

I'd like to thank Jonathan Karp, whose editorial contributions were most welcome (not to mention helpful) and whose respect for writers made me feel very protected.

Finally, I'd like to thank the most Reverend Barry Hirsch, whose legal and personal wisdom, along with his friendship, have always helped me steer a true course.

If you enjoyed

Death by Hollywood,

don't miss these

acclaimed showbiz

novels . . .

The Edgar, Tony, and Grammy award-winning virtuoso of pop entertainment strikes again . . . with his first novel

WHERE THE TRUTH LIES
by
Rupert Holmes

"Sexy and surprising, witty and intriguing."
—Candace Bushnell, author of *Sex and the City*

"A narcotically addictive thriller."
—*Esquire*

"A giddy fun-house ride through bygone eras."
—*The New York Times Book Review*

For more information, go to
www.rupertholmes.com

Published by Random House
Available wherever books are sold